Praise for The Cut Line

"*The Cut Line* revolves around the inner life of a young woman who has recently ended an abusive, toxic relationship. Carolina Pihelgas creates a depth that would not be possible without her poetic language. An extraordinary book by one of Estonia's greatest prose writers today." —*Estonian Literary Magazine*

"Carolina Pihelgas delves deep, peers to the very bottom, is bold and confident, and never stops halfway." —PIRET PÕLDVER, literary critic

The Cut Line

CAROLINA PIHELGAS

The Cut Line

Translated from the Estonian
by Darcy Hurford

WORLD EDITIONS
New York

Published in the USA in 2026 by World Editions NY LLC, New York

World Editions
New York

Copyright © 2024 by Carolina Pihelgas

Original title *Lõikejoon*

First published in 2024 by Loomingu Raamatukogu
English translation copyright © Darcy Hurford, 2026
Author portrait © Natalia Balanina

This book has been supported by the Cultural
Endowment of Estonia, Traducta program

Printed by Lightning Source, USA

Library of Congress Cataloging in Publication Data is available

ISBN 978-1-64286-161-7

Company: worldeditions.org
Facebook: @WorldEditionsInternationalPublishing
Instagram: @WorldEdBooks
TikTok: @worldeditions_tok
Twitter: @WorldEdBooks
YouTube: World Editions

The reflection of the first knife
I ever dreamt of was in my hand again

ARIANA HARWICZ
(TRANS. SARAH MOSES AND CAROLINE ORLOFF)

The knife is long and blunt; it cannot cut. It's spent too long lying in the kitchen drawer and no one's touched it in ages. I press it against my skin, but all it leaves is a white mark that soon disappears. Can't cut meat; can't kill people. How I've longed to press a knife against your throat and hiss angrily like a snake. But not this knife. A blunt knife's no use to anyone. Not to anyone but me. Maybe I'll bury it later, under the apple tree. But maybe I'll carefully press it into my throat and slide it down or spin around and fly into the forest. No, I can't do that. Under the weight of the knife I collapse, I shatter into splinters, into fragile glass.

Along with the knife, I've been left with a drawerful of plastic spoons—nothing could be duller and more pointless—and two or three wasps' nests in the attic. I look around the kitchen of my new home, see the remnants of an old life that are now useless, and immediately I feel at home. My life's also useless and I've left it behind.

I take a few bundles of things inside, but don't start unpacking immediately. Instead, I go and dig the garden for an hour, in a completely arbitrary patch in the yard. This is a time-honored method of banishing thoughts. After that I sit at the kitchen table, drink water from the well and see what else is in the drawers, which have gathered a lot of clutter over the years. I breathe. I breathe again. And already I'm hearing your voice.

All the words you've ever said to me, melting together disgustingly, all the garbled, synthesized phrases aimed solely at hurting me. Well, look at yourself, just look at yourself. Why shouldn't you be happy, you've got everything! Turning on the waterworks again, first thing in the morning. What's wrong with you, just what is wrong with you?

Meanwhile, I couldn't take the car out of town; I wanted to drive myself to oblivion too badly. Things aren't much better now, although I've taken to my heels, with a temporary excuse to start with. Temporary solutions are like duct tape, though, meant to last forever, and your reproachful voice still sounds inside me because I know damn well what you would say about every single thing.

After digging, I decide to mow the lawn in front of the house, all of its flowering clover. As short as possible. I know you wouldn't approve, because you hate mowing the lawn, but that's exactly why I'm doing it. That way, this place will be a little more mine. It'll give me a long-missed feeling of satisfaction, although more out of schadenfreude than anything else. A harmless schadenfreude, because the grass will grow back. And a secret one too, because no one except me will see it.

In the end I could no longer withstand your gaze—or my own—because of what poured out of you; a constant assessment of what you deemed good and adequate. Although in fact the tyrannical judge lives on inside me and maybe you have nothing to do with it.

Tsõriksoo is a tiny cottage farm and the last person who really lived here was my great-aunt Elvi, whom I don't remember at all. Which means a lot of time has gone by. When she couldn't manage on her own anymore she was put in a nursing home, where she died not long afterwards. Then, when Elvi was gone, some urgent repairs were made to the house: a lot of trash was taken away and new floors were laid, sometimes on top of what had been bare earth. After that, we started going there sometimes in summer according to some unwritten schedule.

That was more than twenty years ago. Back when everything around here was still calm; back when I was still a child. Oh I remember those summers. Later I took a break from visiting for a while, when everything else seemed more interesting than the old farmhouse. A few years ago I started again, although it annoyed me that I was still treated like a child, that there was always a list of jobs waiting for me that had to be done. You can't just sit there twiddling your thumbs. Just a few little jobs, nothing much. Mom's lists were always like reproaches.

And then you. All those times when you were there, I realized that when I was with you, nothing really belonged to me. You hated nature, all those annoying insects and discomforts, couldn't stand farm work and would much rather have been sitting at your desk in town in safe isolation, listening to jazz. But you also couldn't stand the idea that I could manage somewhere on my own, without you, couldn't bear the feeling of being set aside. And so you sipped tea in front of the house, sipped and listened to birdsong and read a book while I rushed around working, carrying logs or whatever. Or fence posts, to be exact, but that doesn't matter. You looked on with a condescending smirk. You didn't help.

I should have realized that you were trying to punish me, but it's only now that I'm starting to understand it all. When I didn't behave the way you liked, the way I should, then punishment followed—for example, because I didn't want to sleep with you anymore. I'd started keeping my distance, but still your big paws tried to get through my clothes, touching my body at unexpected moments; you wanted to cross the boundary I had begun to set. Of course it hurt you that I wanted to separate myself from you, to split my self from yours. Because you still considered me a part of you, you didn't see and didn't want to comprehend, so when I dared to refuse, you took offense and began to think up little punishments. Sometimes you wouldn't speak to me for several days. Or, on the contrary, you would ridicule me, not arbitrarily, but with a refined attempt at humiliation, in precisely the way that would hurt as much as possible.

The day I told you I was leaving, I asked if you even understood how much you'd hurt me with your words. You just smirked and admitted with some pride that you were pretty good at it, yes. Inside me, something finally caved in.

So now I'm here by myself. I left you. I told you I had a few things I needed to think over, by myself. Luckily you don't have a driver's license, so you can't show up at the door unexpectedly, and the bus only comes once a week. And now here I am. The cuckoos are calling, the bees buzzing, the birch leaves fluttering in the wind like a hope, like a promise, like something that wishes it could speak.

I wake in the morning to the rattling of automatic guns. Shots are being fired. Not very far away; not very close by either. It's eight o'clock. I can't sleep anymore. Every shot sounds like it's coming from within, from the fear of what's inside me. I draw back the curtains and bright light pours in through the dirty window: a new day that I instantly loathe, as I can't do anything with it. The bedroom is in the old pantry, the darkest room. There's only one narrow window in here. But outside there are apple trees, which for some reason aren't blossoming even though it's the season, and ground elder that's getting taller. Looking at trees is good: branches, leaves, movement. There's a hole inside the trunk of one old apple tree. If I couldn't see that it was growing green leaves, I wouldn't believe a tree like that could be alive. A small child or an animal could easily fit into that hollow. It's like an organ pipe the wind might play at night, just as it plays wildly in elevator shafts and ravines. The hollow bones of dead birds would make small slender pipes; these sounds are sharp, barely audible. Maybe inside my head, which doesn't want to be silent, I'm vibrating—which means I'm an instrument too.

My muscles are stiff and slightly sore. I go outside and listen to the wind. The sun warms my skin, the grass is fragrant and the gunfire has stopped for a moment. I would like simply to sit in the sun and watch the branches moving in the wind and not think about anything. For this lightness to last and not be crushed by my own thoughts. But already I know that soon something will push me and make me act.

A large fly waddles across the outhouse wall, drowsy and content. I am the large fly's antagonist. I take a chair outside but only sit there for a moment as I can't keep still. I grab my gardening gloves and begin pulling the weeds out from around the flowering quince. I haven't done any weeding for years, but I discover that nettles are the nicest; pulling them out by the roots feels so agreeable. Dandelions are annoying, whereas ground elder is easy to pull out. Perhaps you only let me go without much of a fight because you don't believe I'll stay here longer than just a weekend. You probably don't believe I have any right to break up with you. I'm just like a part of your body you feel incomplete without. But what do I feel? Right now simply panic, I guess. I'd known for a long time that I needed to get away, but also that you wouldn't let me go that easily, that it was the departure that scared me the most, the anger and rage that would start building up inside you, swelling and swelling and then exploding and pushing their nasty roots inside me. I'm afraid that when I turn on my phone the day after tomorrow to connect my laptop to the internet—because it'll be Monday and I'll need to start answering work emails—that there'll be messages from you. If you don't know what your hand is doing, cut it off! I'm thinking this by the woodpile, where nettles proliferate from every possible opening, and I pick up the old ax. The blade wobbles. I put it in a water barrel, like Mom taught me. I'll be needing it.

I was eighteen and had just left home. I was taking a year off and working in a call center. It was tedious work, but it paid well. We had to make hotel reservations for Brits, and sometimes early in the morning calls from America were put through to us. People never understood they weren't speaking directly with the hotel. The worst thing was the constant talking, you had to keep chattering for eight hours a day, which meant it was nice to keep quiet the rest of the time. On the weekends I went to concerts, bars, or just hung out and tried to figure out what I liked. I had lots of acquaintances, I had great roommates, but no real friends. My need for closeness was so great that when we met at a party in the early hours of the morning and you told me we were going to your place like it was something completely obvious, I simply followed along without hesitation. Besides, you lived so close by, practically around the corner. You had a narrow apartment in the old town, with two rooms to pass through before the tiny kitchen at the very back. There was nowhere to wash and the toilet was in the corridor. Soon I gave up my rented room, took a few of my things with me, and moved in with you. And half a year later, when I went to university, you moved with me to Tartu and we rented our first real home. For some reason I never used to question the fact that you were fifteen years older than me and much wiser and experienced at everything. So why did you choose me? Once you said you liked my wounded expression. You never talked about your own wounds, although I could sense them. But something connected us, something that made us inseparable for a good many years. We merged into each other until neither of us knew where one began and the other ended. And people thought we were a really sweet couple—those were my classmates' exact words: you're such a sweet couple. I needed someone to rescue me, someone who'd pick me up and show me I was loveable. And looking back at those early years, I realize you really did love me. And I loved you. But that wasn't enough.

I'm all sweaty and angry—the scythe is blunt. I'm trying to cut the grass behind the house; the cow parsley is already up to my hips. Mostly it's cow parsley, but also thistles and burdock. Maybe I should just leave things be, like before. But for some reason I always have this need to act. I hack and hack away and it's like my life: I try to force myself through something. I'm panting. I want space around me, I want a horizon that promises things might change.

Later I take a bowl of water outside and pour it over myself. I go and look at the fruit trees. They should have been blossoming ages ago. All the leaves on the apple trees have holes in them. I notice clusters of yellow-green worms inside the netting—some pest, I suppose. I take a picture to google later. The trees are all unpruned too, the crowns a long way up in the distance. They won't yield a single apple. The cherry trees around the pond are young and still have their leaves, but the branches are swarming with ants and aphids. I don't know why Aunt Tiina even planted these cherries, because the birds usually eat the whole crop before anyone gets to them anyway. I'm not going to start buying apples from the shop though. Damn nature. Nasty pests. The feeling of powerlessness that had just started to fade now returns in full force. Damn it all.

This place got out of hand long ago. It always happens to places when no one lives there for years on end and there's more than one owner. The land and the house are suitable for habitation though, the well has enough water to manage on, and everything's growing abundantly. The only downside is the neighbors, the noisy ones. When the last major expansion of the military training area took place, a while back, we were in danger of losing the house. Mom would always call me in the evenings and tell me what she'd heard somewhere, the stories spreading like wildfire, and ask dramatically if the house would be taken from us. I asked whether it was such a bad thing, maybe it was for the best. She hadn't really ever wanted to live here. I could tell she was on the verge of tears. I understand that there's a war on, she said, but must there be a war on our own people too? Was there no other way? Why can't they be happy with what they already have?

Initially they promised that the government would buy up everything and pay generous compensation. But then things started dragging out as usual, and eventually, when the final boundaries were fixed and it was reported in the news, it turned out that our village would be partially excluded from the extension. The defense minister spoke in person and said our hundred-and-twenty-year-old village would escape destruction. Though everything here's dying anyway. And maybe I didn't know whether to be happy or sad about the news either. For sure, it's nice that the house is still here, but no one knows how it's all going to turn out in the end.

After a while they started talking about another extension. The new boundaries weren't completely final, they said, so if people came to a mutual understanding and agreed to sell everything off as one larger piece of land, they would buy it. Meetings were held, big and small, official and unofficial, and of course there were some who weren't prepared to leave at all, as well as some who wanted the money to start over somewhere else, somewhere quieter. There were divisions, quarrels; there was badmouthing and complaining. The air grew heavy.

And because the house might have to be given up, no one lifted a finger to maintain it. What for? It was all meaningless, as if it were floating in the air. Before, my uncle would still cut the grass and repair the shed roof; now ground elder and nettles are growing everywhere, and it's full of cow parsley and bindweed. Luckily the roof of the house is still intact, the walls are still standing, the birds still sing and the peonies are coming out, the pink buds emerging from the hay like every year.

When everything is quiet, when the guns aren't firing, this is the most beautiful place in the world.

Finally tiredness comes. I make up the bed and eat boiled potatoes at the table with chives and salt. Isn't this the kind of peaceful evening I was dreaming of? There's a large oak outside the window, under the oak there are tulips in flower, and in the distance the cow parsley is already gleaming. There's an interesting exotic tree here, with a beautiful crown and long fine branches. I wonder who planted it? Long bluish-pink stripes stretch across the sky. Mosquitos bump against the windows almost audibly. I can still hear my own breathing. I hear the fork striking the plate and clattering onto the table. And then I'm in a place where nothing moves forward anymore, everything only goes backward, turns back on itself, tells me about the meaninglessness of my existence. Reality is a snake coiling up, but there's no room for me here. I'm excluded from all living things, from all breathing things. Without other people, do I even exist? What happens to a person deep down, right at the bottom, in solitude?

I breathe. I breathe. Is it possible that here in this old house, far from everything, I could turn into something else, into a plant, say? Doesn't that make me like something that's poked its head out of the ground; something pale green that's stretched out, caught some sun, maybe even managed to grow some flowers, but not borne fruit? And is then cut down and trampled to pieces. Don't I have roots, then, somewhere deeper still? I should just go back to bed, curl up under the blanket and cry a bit. I need to stay beneath the soil, in the ground, here in a safe remote place until I find the strength within me to sprout new shoots.

And maybe I'm just a child, only now starting to utter its first words and make some sense of things. I put off talking to you because it would've meant admitting that I'd done too much harm to myself. That I was stuck, that I couldn't face reality. The reality wasn't you; it was us.

What else were those long periods of self-absorption where I tried to suppress everything external; a sort of dying within the emptiness. Mirrors made me want to kill the tired woman looking back at me. She seemed hopeless.

Maybe I believed that suffering was a way to reach something I've been really longing for, that suffering would take me past the surface to somewhere beyond, but now I realize I was just deceiving myself. It was cowardice. I didn't have the strength to act, but in the end there was no other choice.

I'm still afraid that my words are empty and don't mean anything, point nowhere.

At night I die several times.

Monday morning arrives with listlessness. A lack of sleep has shut down my responses. I get up and pretend I can walk on two legs. It still feels good taking the few steps from bed to garden, into the sun, wind and air. The grass is still cold and dewy, but the sun gleams mercilessly. The forecast is drought, sultry. I like warmth but I don't want to see everything dry up and turn yellow.

I take the buckets, go to the well, put water on to boil for coffee, and switch on my laptop at the kitchen table. While I'm waiting for it to start up, the adrenaline kicks in, because I want to know what you have to say to me, yet don't at the same time. First of all I look at work emails. There are plenty of them, so I'll be busy all day. And then my personal emails. You've sent me five emails over the weekend. I can't open them right away so I stand up, my heart thudding, my throat constricting with anxiety, and I pour hot water over the coffee grounds and take the milk out of the fridge. I try to take deep breaths. Then I sit back down and read your messages as quickly as possible to take in all the nastiness at once, and then quickly close the mailbox again.

I touch my face, hair, eyes, cheeks—what do I look like? What you describe in your emails is not me. It's someone else, some image you've created in your head that has nothing to do with me. It's scary. Did I spend fourteen years with a person who didn't even see me?

You say you don't understand why I had to go away. That everything was fine. That you're waiting for me to come back and could I come as soon as possible.

And then in the second email you say I'm a senseless stupid bitch. And then that you were just a bit upset and a little drunk, which of course is my fault, seeing as I left you in such a vulnerable position, but we could still get together and discuss things. That the door to your heart is still open to me. That no one else will want me anyway and what's more, why break something that has worked so well until now, has been nothing but great and wonderful.

All of that. Your words are absolutely ridiculous and yet they eat away at me. You really do think I belong to you.

You trample me into the dirt, trying to crush me one last time. I freeze and cover my head with my arms as if struck by invisible blows, like it doesn't matter that you're a hundred kilometers away.

But then anger comes welling up.

It comes from deep within, an anger I've never dared to feel before. It's a wild feeling of injustice that I've been treated like an inferior kind of being that doesn't deserve respect. Like someone who can be pushed around, who can be manipulated, who can be reproached, humiliated, and who won't fight back. Why didn't I fight back? Why did I put up with it all? I'm mad at myself as well. No, hold on a moment. That's another thing that's been planted in me: blame yourself, descend into an endless labyrinth where you find nothing but your own faults. Analyze only what you did wrong. Consider what you did to deserve it. And anyway, if it was so bad, why didn't you leave sooner? Stop.

I inform you laconically that in the future you'll have to cope by yourself, please, I'm not your mother or your property. I'm not coming back anymore, well, I mean, only for a few last things, later on sometime.

I'm not going to respond to the work emails right now. I can't deal with text in this state, so I'm going to go outside with an old sheet and take a pile of logs to the chopping block. I take an ax. The first log is you. I chop you in half with one blow. The second is our relationship. The ax gets stuck—there's a knot in the wood. I strike again and again. There are already long cracks in the wood, but it resists. I'm being drawn into the movement by the weight of the ax blade in my hand. Finally, the log is broken. I'll turn it into little pieces of kindling for the stove.

Then onto the next log. My mom. Somehow always present, but not fully there, a self-centered expression on her face that looks right past me—just don't you embarrass me. Giving the appearance of being caring, but really also wanting to control and meddle as if I existed purely so she could prove her self-worth. I'm going to chop her into splinters. I'm in full swing. I strike a few logs at the same time. Then: Dad, of course. Self-absorbed, silent. The coward who took off. Well, okay, he had a reason. A reason to even forget his children's birthdays eventually. If Mom's the one controlling everything, Dad's a hobbit hiding under the rug. I'm whacking logs with all my might.

My younger sister Pille. Always the favorite. I remember my disappointment as a child when I realized I wasn't the only one anymore, no longer everyone's pet. I bullied Pille and she complained. At some point she started complaining even when I hadn't done anything, just to show her power. This one's for you.

My first boyfriend. Who messed me around, only met up when he felt like it, until in the end he just stopped picking up the phone. A hundred for you.

I gasp and finally stick the ax back into the block. The horseflies and garden flies swirl around me; the smell of sweat drives them crazy. I'm surrounded by a pile of chopped wood. I'm going to pick you up piece by piece and stack you all up. It'll be a tall stack. You'll keep me warm on the chilly fall evenings, should they ever arrive here. It's boiling hot right now. And getting hotter. It hasn't rained in weeks. Even though everything's still green now after a lovely spring, I can feel there's a drought on its way.

A crazy buzzing sound is getting closer. I duck, but then look up. It's not the din of the low-flying fighter planes, but it's still terribly loud and vibrates against my body. Then I see them: two helicopters, flying really low, so low that I can read the letters on their undersides. They're moving towards the polygon, the military area. I remember when I was a kid I liked waving at trains, at boats. Would they wave back at me from the helicopter? Would they even notice me? They must be flying low enough to see me, at least if they were interested—a woman in a long blue flowery dress in her teeny farmhouse yard, chopped wood in her arms and dust in her eyes.

I feel like I'm eighteen again, like the fourteen years in between were a mistake and now I have to resume my life at the same point. Like sliding down the ladder in woolen socks. What did I dream of back then? Impossible to remember. I'd escaped from home. I was very lonely and hoping that someone would show me how life worked. I don't want my youth back, even if I'm not sure I spent it in the most meaningful way. But I am oddly certain that now I need to be here at Tsõriksoo. Even with the helicopters flying above. Even though this little farmhouse is falling apart and the grass is growing above my head and the horsefly bites are painful.

Up until this moment I'd thought that I was only capable of hating myself. So I'm going to spend another few days investigating this recently awakened feeling. I hold the hatred in my hands like a chick, and feel its little heart beating frantically. At some point it'll start flapping its wings about and get bigger than me. Then I'll have to let it go and cover my face. I can't control it entirely.

I keep experiencing unexpected bursts of joy and wild bouts of optimism that can quickly turn into depression. These feelings are tiring. And yet I'm pleased that I can feel something again. It's like a faucet's been turned back on. The water coming out is still dirty, but that's better than nothing at all. I don't trust myself yet. But I'm reading all kinds of articles about leaving relationships that repeat the mantra: give yourself time. I should start giving myself time, and everything else, too. Understanding. Care.

I message a friend. I need proof that I'm sane. I can write about it now, but I still can't talk about it. Yet I need to know that someone's on my side. Meanwhile I'm beginning to question if I really made the right decision. We were together for such a long time, after all. What if he's right that no one else would have a use for me. Doubt is like a cobweb—very delicate, but when you touch it, it clings to your fingers. Gray and sticky.

The dial points at me and I feel like I'm to blame. Before I left, you told me I was selfish, self-absorbed. That I was incapable of love. Well maybe I am. Maybe our relationship turned sour because of me! Maybe I failed to support you, maybe I wasn't good enough, however hard I tried. Or I wasn't as responsive as I could have been, didn't take care of you, of our home. But I just wasn't able to.

Just like my mom wasn't able to love me. That's why I'm a broken sound. The swallows are flapping around in the sky. Death is a woman, but with whose face?

I'm gradually getting used to the loud humming of the old fridge, the nice view from the bedroom window of the eaten-away apple trees, and the birches growing in the distance.

I pull the wax tablecloth off the kitchen table. The wood underneath is beautiful. If anyone says anything, I'll replace it with a new one. I can't stand wax tablecloths. They remind me of my childhood, when everything was covered in slippery flowery patterns to protect things from people. When so much was forbidden, when children were always in the way; always too noisy, restless, demanding. Children disturbed adults' peace. Which meant we were sent outdoors pretty often and we had the freedom to prowl and loaf around. But we also understood we were superfluous and troublesome.

Being here awakens strange fantasies in me. That it would be nicer if the walls were soda blasted inside. The rosehip bush behind the house could be rooted out. The shady area that is currently the dung heap could be emptied, the trash taken to the waste station, the metal framework covered in plastic film, and a greenhouse built. A new fridge would be a good idea and a real stove instead of this portable mini stove with only one hob. But then I shake myself out of it: you're only here temporarily. Don't get involved: you're not staying here forever, just this summer. Worst-case scenario, into September. At some point you're going back to the city, you can't live in perpetual fear of that man.

I don't have a future now. Something has ended, but a new life hasn't yet begun. In its own way, the lack of plans is liberating. I can work on a laptop from more or less anywhere. Maybe I really should spend winter in southern Europe? Andalusia or Sicily, one of the Greek islands? But I don't have the strength to go anywhere far away on my own. And what would I do over there, all by myself? Traveling sounds lovely, but the idea of getting through it gives me the shivers.

Because I'm coping as it is. I can't keep on fleeing.

One east-facing window is full of weird stripes. I clean them off in the evening. And seeing as I'm already holding a newspaper and cleaning materials, I do a round of the whole house. When I make it back to the first window, it's full of greasy marks again. I wash it clean again and go inside, throw myself on the couch and lie there, waiting. Soon I hear a dull thud. And another one. And another. It's a big dark bird, probably a blackbird, trying to get inside, chest-first. He flies desperately into the window, hurls himself against the glass. What kind of madness is that? What's he even looking for? The house hardly resembles a nest, and even if it did, it would be too large for him. A rustle of wings, some panicked movements, and then he flies away. I neither know who he was nor understand what he wanted.

I haven't seen another human in a week. It's getting weird, but luckily I do need to go to the store. I get out the old bike and pump up the tires and I bike the six kilometers to the village store. Apart from a couple of work-related phone calls, I realize I haven't spoken to anyone. The first thing I do is stop by the magazine racks and check out the covers. It feels like the colorful pictures on the covers are from a different world entirely, from a different plane of existence. There are newspapers too. I weigh up whether to buy *Õhtuleht* but decide against it. Aunt Tiina only reads *Õhtuleht* and she says it has all the most accurate news and it's the only paper where they write about things as they really are. That kind of certainty is appealing, but I disagree. Apart from me, there are two small boys buying bread, sausage and ice cream, and a middle-aged man stocking up on beer cans in the cold store. I'm glad to see the oranges. And the ice cream. How banal I've become!

When I say hi and thanks to the cashier, I feel as if I'm squawking.

I cycle home with a heavy backpack but in a good mood. The crops are sprouting and swaying in the wind: long waving fields, tiny little houses, pale clouds in a bright sky. The landscape here is so familiar yet foreign, all these bends in the road rising and falling, the avenue of oaks that gives way to the houses, the silhouette of the brick factory. As kids we were afraid that it was haunted. But mainly just the billowing fields, and far behind them the forest. It pulsates as if opening from within.

When I unpack everything in the kitchen, a surge of pain hits me. Starting at my feet, it comes through my soles as a tingling and then it rapidly spreads throughout my body. In panic, I clutch the edge of the table and I look up instinctively because now the whole house is shaking and I'm afraid it could come down on my head. Should I run outside or hide under the table? I don't have time to do anything. I freeze. It lasts a brief moment and then it's over, but it feels like my feet are still vibrating. Or is it coming from inside me? I go outside and everything is as before. But my heart's pounding like fury. It must have been an explosion. The second time it happens, I'm outside, and the surge of pain is the same. An image comes to me of the earthworms being crushed, the soil torn up, smoke and soot spreading everywhere. My house hasn't collapsed. But I fall onto the soft green grass, face-first on the cool clover, arms and knees outstretched like an anchor that's too far from the seabed.

Mom rings. Enquires how I am. And whether I've mown the grass yet. And whether I haven't mown too much, because of the drought. And what are my plans for Midsummer, as she and aunt Tiina are thinking of coming out to the countryside too. I must have realized that they're afraid I can't handle things in this place, that I'm making a mess of things. I'd like to say to her that I don't have any plans at all for life in general, but I answer simply that if you want to come then do. It would be great. A family Midsummer, when was the last time one of those happened … maybe fourteen years ago? Probably. I'm just getting my fingers around a peppermint bush when Mom starts saying how she's already planning what meat to bring for the barbecue and what kind of salad to make, and asks me if there's chives, if I haven't accidentally mown them away. And if I've planted anything myself or maybe been too caught up in my own stuff or—what am I even doing there? I say I work a bit and relax a bit, everything's fine, I'll make the salad and fresh pickled cucumbers myself, you prepare whatever else we need.

I'm imagining her already starting to make lists.

The phone call makes me feel both safe and anxious. One part of the world is very much still standing, but it was precisely the part I thought I'd never break away from as a teenager. Now that I'm an adult back in that childhood world, I should be equal to my parents, yet I'm not, not really. I'm still somehow in debt to them. I'm an item on a list that needs to be taken care of. Closeness comes at a price; it's not given for free.

I shudder. From somewhere far away, a roaring sound's approaching. But it's just the neighbor's tractor along the dusty gravel road. We still have some farms with proper country people who live here all year round, not just summer guests. There used to be a few who kept beef cattle here, but the pasture ended up underneath the military extension, while the houses were spared. They didn't move away, though. They rented land from somewhere else or crammed things together on the land they had left. Half the people around here must still be on antidepressants.

I remember a news broadcast from a couple of years back, where an old woman talked tearfully to a reporter about how she didn't want to move anywhere and nor did she want any money. The only thing she did want was to die peacefully in her own home. What happened to her? Was she put in a nursing home? Did a younger relative take her in? Did she die of distress?

No rain is on its way. The air's hot and flickers and twitches at my temples.

The tension's starting to ease up. As if I've left a heavy sack of flour behind me in the city, one that I'd been dragging behind me for years. I've started sleeping better and I'm breathing more easily. It's not all over yet, from time to time a compulsion or fear hits me, but now I'm finding there are small moments where I'm not worrying about anything, where I can simply listen to the birds tweeting or look at the sunflowers which have grown a couple of centimeters taller overnight. I want to shake my body, throw off the pressure that's accumulated on my skin, scrub off all the muck. What will be left? It's dangerous to be something shapeless that can be taken to pieces. I haven't put together a new body yet.

I'm thinking about the imagined lives I've lived in the last few years, the longing to be somewhere else, with someone else. To be someone else. For years I was nothing but longing. Fear drove me—fear of that moment when I might look back and see empty longing instead of a life properly lived. And yet I have doubts: the thing inside me manically overthinking and desperately running after solitude—is it still me? Or is it something else, someone else?

Those questions aren't just thin air now. They have reality, substance and character.

I don't know if coming to Tsõriksoo was a new life for great-aunt Elvi as well. Although she must have been over sixty by then. She was a spinster with no children. Worked in the town library and then came here to take care of another old woman. It could also have been out of necessity, not choice; you never know. But it was near the end of the Soviet era, so it could hardly be something really terrible anymore. I should ask Mom—I actually don't know very much about Elvi.

It's good to get up from the computer now and then and go outside. I remember how, as children, we were made to pick and clean currants here, how annoying it was. I remember having fun jumping on hay bales with my sister and playing around, how we buried the baby birds that fell from their nests under the apple trees, how we decorated their graves with braided wreaths. The secret hut beneath a large spruce at the edge of the forest. I know someone who grew up in the country and who categorically refuses to weed flowerbeds. I feel no such reluctance. But then there hasn't really been a proper household at Tsõriksoo since Elvi's time.

At night I walk to the edge of the forest. The sky's still glowing the color of sunset, but the forest's already almost dark. The mosquitoes whine. This is their favorite time of day. The shadows of the trees are long and a little lonely. I want to shake off a day full of words and meanings. Not that they're superfluous, just that I don't need them anymore. I rustle through the scrub, dry branches crackling under my feet. Walking back to the house, I give a start. There's an evil grunt. And there he is: eyes glowing, teeth gleaming. Ready to gobble me up. My fear, ready to engulf me. I close my eyes and say, Take me. He growls for a bit longer but doesn't come any closer. Tired, he lies down, puts his muzzle on his paws and shuts his eyes.

In the morning my eyelids are heavy. I was longing to feel alone; and now the feeling's here. Time stretches out, leaves me by myself. Sometimes I'd like the morning to just keep going, the coffee in the cup not to run out, the sentence not to end, the dandelion seeds to keep flying. To be in a photographic silence where everything keeps going but doesn't end.

Though wasn't I alone even when I was with you? Alone when I needed support, alone when I was struggling with depression and haunted by memories, alone planning vacations and looking for hotels, alone shouldering everyday responsibilities. Alone when you punished me with silence and withdrew into your bubble, and I had to guess what I'd done wrong. I was alone when I was a kid, and I was alone with you too. But the solitudes I've lived with my whole life are different from now in so many ways; my aloneness now is a little easier. It contains a longing for connection, but no desire to please—and no demanding tone or prying questions from you.

I've started listening to podcasts so I don't forget human speech and don't forget words. I didn't ever think I'd spend so long by myself. It's like sailing on the ocean for weeks on end: you know that dry land exists, but you still feel a bit dubious. The garden's a good companion. I watch the plants grow, bud, straighten their backs, and bloom. I'm trying to figure out which plants I've sown and which are weeds. And I water, of course, I water.

When I was little, I loved beetles, which there were plenty of here. And I hated the ants. I still don't like them. I'm not scared of them biting me anymore, but I can't stand them climbing on the peonies. I googled and found out that they even drink sap from the buds. A few ants wouldn't matter, but there are absolutely loads of them here. Which feels suspect somehow. In general, the ants try to climb up on everything in the garden, they really are getting more like people. On the cherry trees they graze on aphids, and I notice now that the blackcurrant bush is crawling with suspicious amounts of them; they have nests inside the woodpiles where they climb along your splintered legs and arms and groin, they are under practically every stone, not to mention along the edge of the sauna house, where there are whole colonies. Big and small, black and red, whole legions of ants. This is a strange empire where the ants' rules apply, where battles are fought and possessions won from each other. Small soldier insects, ready to take over the world. Just as long as they don't break into the house. I no longer want to share my room with anyone.

I have my work: letters, sentences, texts, meanings. But I also have slowly passing clouds, shadows swaying over trees, and frogs' wedding songs in the pond. Or maybe they have me. Maybe in some strange way I'm here as a witness, a companion, a pair of eyes. Maybe the land owns me and makes me act, makes me move and take care, lets me cry, crawl, sweat and breathe.

Early in the morning I turn on the radio, and it's the news again, nothing but news all the time, telling me nothing new because the war's still going on as well as the drought. One piece of crap news after another. I tune out the news, find a station playing old songs, a safe backdrop from a time when everything had already begun to stink, when people were already saying we were heading for shit creek, but there weren't that many people listening. If two hundred species die out in one day, how many will that amount to in my lifetime? The thought makes me want to give up and die. The news depresses me like anyone else—it's all too hard to take in. I want a safe bubble to float in. Not to be ignorant of what is going on, but so I don't have to deal with it all the time. And at the same time, passivity frightens me. The apparent sense of security that comes from enclosing myself in my tiny bubble frightens me.

My hands are empty, but I dream of a knife to cut through the thin veil of indifference.

And in a weird way, I still feel guilty. Maybe it was just me the whole time. Maybe I didn't know how to keep a relationship going, didn't know how to open up fully. Maybe something in me was broken, and I'm so badly damaged by my suffering that I'm poisoning everything around me as well.

Shortly before I leave for town, I see a fox beside the well. A young one, looking around curiously. I pause. I want to look at it a little longer. It's a beautiful fox, but with a scraggy tail. It sniffs, then stops again with one paw raised, alert and vigilant. It listens. I don't want to scare it, but I need to get going, so I take a couple of steps into the yard and then it finally runs off. I don't know if it was a sign and if so, whether that's good or bad.

Before I drive off, I look at myself in the small mirror in the car. My skin's already slightly tanned, and there are some worry lines on my forehead and two mosquito bites at the temples. The look in my eyes is tired, but not broken.

We sit in the café. I've had breakfast here occasionally, when we were arguing or you weren't talking to me, and the air was heavy with feelings. Today the place is pretty busy and the only free table is in the middle of the room. I order just coffee; I can't eat with this tension. It's half past nine. Why are there so many people here?

I just don't understand, is the first thing you say. I look past you. Away from those familiar eyes that can be loving one moment and full of anger the next. From the facial features I know, from the head, the greasy hair that's started going gray. The air is stuffy, all breathed up. There's a small vase in the middle of the table with a cutting that's growing roots, and a small round lace doily underneath. I'd like to touch it, but then I'd be too close to you. I squeeze the armrests of the chair I'm sitting on. My sigh is a little too loud, but I ask very quietly: so what don't you understand? Well, you say, why do you need to do all this, this crap, this performance? You think you're kind of special, don't you? What the hell are you up to? I look away again, the waiter brings us two cups, and I keep quiet. What am I even doing here? What do I have to tell you? That I've suffered and that all this is a trap. When were we thrown into this trap? What's it doing to us? The spoons clink against the cups. The saucers are ideal, perfectly round. Your tea is steaming. You open the little jar of honey and empty it sharply into the cup. Your movements are angular and nervous; you're losing control of something. Of me. You ask me if I even realize how horribly I'm acting, how selfish I'm being. Destroying it all, just because she's bored. As if he's suddenly not good enough anymore. Do you think you'll find something better somewhere else? If you want to throw away all the great and wonderful things we have, then you're just crazy. Or even worse, stupid. Can't even call you young and stupid now—just stupid. His voice has become a whisper, a sotto voce that carries more than normal speech. I look around. There's a young man with headphones on by the window at a laptop. At the table next to him two older ladies are eating cake. So early in the morning, I think, I wonder how they manage it. They keep talking, a little louder, not turning their heads. Your intensity pins me to the spot. Do you really think anyone would want you? you ask. Look at yourself, look what you're like, just one massive failure. Best steer well clear. But I don't want to throw away all these years. Do you even understand, fourteen years, that's no joke. Look at everything we've done together. All those great things. And anyway, what are you hoping to achieve? Two weeks you've been out there in the countryside, is that not enough? I'll still take you back now. But soon the door will shut and that's it, it's over. You listening?

What is it, not good enough am I, not good enough to talk to?

I barrel out of the café, my hands shaking, and I'm not sure I said a single word.

There are a couple of good shady benches in the botanical garden, one of which I sit down on. I look over at the pond as if from far away: a bird's eye view. It's strange being in town. I'm much more aware of the traffic noise than I used to be. I'd like to crawl into a hole and not be here among people. But I can't allow myself that right now, so I sit and breathe, a soft male voice in my headphones. Breathing helps: the long steady flow of air along the trachea, count to eight, then eight again, until the warm air is expelled. The tremor inside of me doesn't completely go away, but it retreats a little.

I take a little stroll around and look at the plants. Not with innocent eyes. My mom once told me that she'd always found that stolen cuttings grew the best. I wonder if I could gather seeds here. Or how about taking this beautiful Swiss pinecone with me? I stick my hands in my pockets. The moss is so lovely. And the peonies here are miles prouder than mine—they're practically bursting into flower. But I still prefer the wildness and the crazy bustle of my garden, which I'm not really trying to tame.

After lunch I steel myself and decide to go to your place to pick up the last few things: some books, Grandma's vase, a couple of houseplants ... I hold my breath as I turn the key in the door. I'm hoping you're at work. There's silence in the apartment. Fuggy air— someone's been smoking in here. Empty wine bottles. Plants unwatered. I should have taken the bonsai with me sooner, as its leaves have dropped off. The cactus I once gave you for your birthday I'll leave here, it'll survive anywhere. I don't want any pointless arguments about who owns what. I look around the apartment—so many memories, there's some in every corner. Shoo! I scare them away. And it helps: when I close the door behind me, all I have left is ghosts. I put the keys in your mailbox. That's all I need to do. That's something.

A couple of hours later I fall into a friend's place with a bottle of wine, a melon, and a stinging feeling in my throat that I've failed in life.

Silja sits me down on the couch, starts boiling the kettle for tea, and lets me ramble through everything that's been going on these past few weeks. Her presence reminds me there are safe spaces, soft words, friendship. I'm grateful to her for that.

She's a photographer and she's recently started taking cyanotypes, going to the banks of the river Emajõgi and taking pictures of bushes, and then printing abstract blue nature pictures.

But just think, now you can do whatever you want, Silja says, you're free. And I wonder if that feeling of freedom is what's squeezing my chest so hard. Or is all this pain too great, too present, too obvious. Silja says it's grief, you need to grieve, something's ended and ending hurts too. The future I'd imagined together with Tarmo drowned, sank to the bottom and no longer exists. The most awful thing about breakups is losing what you imagined. As ever, Silja's right. The path I'd been following for fourteen years turned out to be a dead end, and now I have to take a few steps sideways to get an idea of what direction to move in.

We talk about loneliness and disappointments, how we imagined ourselves when we were young, and how the relationships we witnessed in childhood weren't good role models. On the contrary, you spend the rest of your life trying to get over them. I tell Silja about how I was bullied at school for being clumsy, slow, and just different. There was an odd number of students in our class, and I sat by myself. I would spend hours after school looking for my jacket and schoolbag, feeling the other kids watching me. When I finally told my mom, she laughed at me. Look what you're doing. Don't attract their attention. Fight back. I was scared of school but scared of Mom too. Because some things upset her so much she would shut herself in her bedroom until the morning and wouldn't open the door even when we were crying for her to do it. And I never knew what would upset her, at least not when I was a kid. Later I learned to read the signs better.

Dad was as incapable of handling it all as I was. He was helpless. Until he finally figured the best solution was to get out of there. But I coped. And I took care of Pille too, I took money for groceries from Mom's purse when she happened to be at home. When she wasn't there, I searched through her coat pockets to find any coins she'd left. I was so anxious. I was shouldering burdens that weren't mine. And then I picked a man who was just as unpredictable, just as closed, just as emotionally helpless.

You can stay here for a couple of days if you want, Silja says. I feel so happy to hear this. Right now I just really need someone to care about me.

Going home the next day I see the fumes from a long way off. Turning onto the village road, I also see the rescue workers: some pumping water from the river, others standing at the roadside with water hoses. The polygon's burning. It always happens when there's a drought. The forest is dry, they have shooting exercises, something catches light, but you can't enter the site to extinguish it as there might be explosives; so they let the forest burn to dark-gray ash, until it reaches the limits. The rescue workers stand at the roadside to see that the fire doesn't spread, but everything inside the boundary will burn. It's not really my end of the polygon, but if the wind's blowing right, the fumes will be carried to Tsõriksoo as well. I just hope it doesn't go on too long and that the fire goes out soon.

I lie down on the lawn in the golden warmth of the evening sun. I look over in the other direction, where the smoke isn't visible. There, on the other side of the trees, are wheat fields. I want to look up at the clouds and just take a break. I'll take my things out of the car soon, but I just need a quiet moment first. The clover under my arms is so soft, the flickering of the aspens is soothing.

What will become of all this? Yesterday's conversations are still burning inside me. Has my whole life just been compulsive repetition? My skin's covered in big bruises, but whose hands put them there? All these fears and silences, wanting to live up to expectations. Whose expectations are they? And is it possible that until now I haven't really been able to trust anyone?

And then something in me springs a leak. I'm scared, I'm a little kid. How old? I'm eight or nine, already in school. I'd like someone to come and give me a cuddle. For someone to look at me and respond, to reassure me that there are people who stand up to malice. That darkness can come from within a person, but so can light. I'm all on my own. No one else is at home. I don't know when Mom'll be home, apparently she's running late. It's afternoon but getting dark already. So as not to be afraid, I turn on all the lights and the cartoon channel on TV, and cuddle my big soft toy dog. Dad gave it to me when I turned six. It came with a collar, a comb and a food bowl. But bad thoughts still pop up. Mom says I don't have a dad anymore. He left us, went away. All that was left was a voice on the phone, who on rare occasions would cheerfully ask me how I was doing. And I don't want to disappoint him, so I answer just as cheerfully, I'm great. I'm wondering, what if I no longer have a mother? What if she doesn't come home? She's drifting away, further and further away from me, floating off on an ice floe. First I can no longer distinguish her features. The further she gets, the more blurred everything becomes. Finally her figure is on the horizon, dark and motionless. I'm completely alone. The stinging pain makes me curl up like a little worm. I still have a little sister and a toy dog, and there are fish in the aquarium. But they're not much use, they need looking after. My little sister shouldn't have anything to worry about. When Mom's at work and I go and pick my sister up from daycare, I need to be wearing a big child's face. The face of someone who's not afraid of anything.

I'm gasping for breath. I'd like to escape, and all the delicious calmness I felt when I arrived in the garden has vanished. My chest is pounding with anxiety and I scream with full force until my strength runs out, until I'm sitting back upright, until my fingers feel the softness of the ground again.

A little emptiness, a little unsteadiness, some joys, some hollows.

There's a dead bird by the far wall of the sauna that must have fallen out of the nest. Or been pushed out. Face twisted in a grimace; the ants have already eaten the eyes in its head. A corpse face. I'm not gathering up the baby bird, not burying it, not putting a wreath of flowers on a tiny grave. I'm not a kid anymore. In a few days this bird will be completely gone. And for some reason, I start thinking about the red clots I give birth to every four weeks, even though they're even less alive, just tiny clots that didn't have even as much chance as that baby bird.

I wanted to fry an egg for lunch but now it seems somehow obscene. I stand at the stove, the egg in my hand and oil heating in the pan. I stand there like a fool and break the egg into the pan anyway. And I eat selfishly. Like someone who's been working hard all day. Like someone who's lost something.

Afterwards I sit in front of the house sipping coffee. The wind wanders gently around the treetops, white wads of cumulus come and go, but the air remains sultry. Still no rain. They've promised a thunderstorm.

At night I'm in my mom and dad's tiny bedroom, my eyes on the wallpaper patterns and curtains. There's a strange emptiness in the room. I'm a kid and I'm sitting in Mom's lap. It's as if everything else was fine, but there's a horrible premonition growing inside me. Quietly I look along the black sweatpants, the ones with three stripes that she always wore, and up to her face. And then to my horror, I see that only Mom's legs are here: from the waist up she's missing, she's invisible, halved. I need her so badly, but she doesn't actually exist. I start to scream, but it's not my voice, just the crying and screaming of a little kid. I feel like I'm about to die. In the midst of this panic I finally realize I'm dreaming and I force myself to move. I wake up. It's four. The anger and loneliness felt so real. They still do. I go to the bathroom. Outside it's already light and the birds are chirping so terribly loudly. The dream is frighteningly accurate: my Mom was only half there for me. For the most part, emptiness stretched out whenever she was present: no eyes to see me, no mouth to speak to me, no ears to listen to me. That small child in the dream was looking for her mother's breast. She wanted milk: warm, safe and nutritious. What would feed me now? And why am I incapable of letting go of my mother?

Seeing your name sends a jolt of fear through me. You've called. I'm not picking up. You're sending me messages. I made a separate folder for them so they wouldn't leap out at me from my inbox. In the meantime I open one, though it's not the wisest idea.

... No one can go it alone. Trees in the forest don't grow alone. Insects don't live alone. Going it alone is such a ridiculous idea that it should be set on fire.

It's so sad that women are like this these days. It's feminism feeding them the idea that they don't need men. And men's commitment is no longer valued at all. All the years we spent together you just threw down the drain. I would have liked to have a child with you. Started a family. We could have really stuck together and created something even more beautiful. I don't even understand what motivated you. Did you get bored? Or was it vanity, the need for attention? Or did you just want to screw around? We could have agreed on something. Probably all three of those things, but maybe there was something else? I repeat: I don't understand. I don't hold any grudge against you, because mostly I'm just furious. I think you're doing things you're going to regret. Unnecessary, pointless actions. But you won't realize that till later, maybe when another fourteen years have passed and it's already too late. Who knows, maybe the regret will be so great you won't even be able to live with it. But still, weren't you getting enough action? Were you that horny?

In one letter you threaten to kill me. That makes me cautious. I wonder how you'd go about it. Force your way into the house, bowie knife in hand, its blade gleaming like the morning sky? Would you be capable of that? I don't think so. Then I remember this actually happened to a former colleague from the call center. It wasn't a break-up, just a jealous man and a family argument. A mist descended before his eyes, he grabbed a knife from the kitchen and stabbed the mother of his children in a rage. He called an ambulance straight after, but Raili died in hospital. Premeditated murder is something else. I weigh whether I should tell the police and decide that if you write anything like that again, I will. What can they do, though? Issue a restraining order? That's no protection against bad intentions. I decide to keep reading the letters every now and then to make sure they don't get any worse.

The lightbulb in the kitchen's blown, and I rummage around trying to find a replacement. There's nothing in the kitchen cupboards. Under the living room window is a moth-eaten dresser which might have been here since the farmhouse was built as it's at least a hundred years old. The drawers don't open properly. Some of the ring pulls are missing and the wood's swollen. And they have every possible sort of thing in them: old papers, keys that no longer open any doors, a Bible in Gothic script, funeral brochures, old German marks—every trace of the house's history and fortunes is here. But no lightbulbs. Carefully I take out yellowed papers and crumbling banknotes that have been kept for some reason. They make me think about the people who've lived here. Elvi, yes, but who else? The plot of land for this small farmhouse was hived off from one of the larger farms and given to a daughter in the family. But when? And why? Was there anything else behind it? Was it to avoid being classed as kulaks?

This house has mostly been run by women—at least that's what I've been told. I find a hymn sheet from a funeral. The name on it is familiar. Selma Raudsepp. Could that be the same woman Elvi came to look after?

It feels like I'm not supposed to be touching these things, like they're too personal, but I push the thought aside. I close the drawer, and slide my hand over the old planks, over the lines and cracks that have appeared over a hundred years. Women have run this farm to the best or worst of their ability and now it's my turn. But I'm not sure I'm a worthy successor in the line. I feel more like a girl than a woman, more like a daughter than an adult. But I'm over thirty and ought to know more about life. Sometimes I feel like I'd rather forget what I know. How am I supposed to find out what really makes me happy, what to be satisfied with? Did the women who lived here know?

I feel like I need a quick dopamine boost, so I quickly post a couple of Insta stories about the flowers in the garden and the evening light and the big oak in front of the house. The hearts start coming, plus a couple of comments. I'd like something more. I'd like to feel that I exist. I'm hiding from the world, true, but I'm still expecting to be found, to be missed. I find myself thinking about different men that I was interested in at some point. Find myself dreaming, even though reason tells me it's too soon to be thinking about such things. I'm alone in my paradise, but a paradise demands to be shared. I'd like to feel someone against me, I'd like someone to caress me, to touch me, to have someone I could look in the eyes, someone's warmth, someone whose embrace I could shiver in, who would kiss my back, neck, nipples, clitoris. I go outside and look for a spot that's sheltered from the wind, put down a rug, and take off my clothes. At least the eternally blazing sun can stroke me, at least there's one thing that can touch me. I rub myself against the rug, press my vulva against the ground and shudder with excitement, my ass facing the sun. I switch on my little pink vibrator and pulsate at its pace, at the pace of the breeze and the swaying haystacks and my own heartbeat and the swallows swirling above me. My head's completely empty: there's no one, no man, no body at all. I'm fully inside myself, in my consciousness, and outside it there's nothing at all; there doesn't need to be anything.

My legs are covered in mosquito bites and my hair hasn't been washed in a week. I need to start getting ready. Midsummer's coming. Mom, Aunt Tiina and Raivo are coming. A storm's coming. The sauna needs to be heated, I need to prove myself and cope with all this. I go to the shop and the market in Võru. To the hardware store as well, because we need mosquito nets and a mole trap. Every morning there's a new mound of earth outside. Luckily there's not much chance of me mowing the grass right now, but I'm cleaning the rooms at least. I wonder if this will be another typical family gathering where tensions are hidden away to start with, but then after a few bottles of wine the accusations start flying. It might start raining too. And does the polygon have a day off at Midsummer? Otherwise there'll be the sound of guns firing all day. You know it's not a real war, but the bangs are still real, and they go right through you for real each time.

Will there soon be summers with no rain, with nothing but drought? Then a brief fall and a long winter. This year, spring only lasted a month and at the end of March it was sleeting—and in May we had the first heatwave already. Here in Tsõriksoo the climate is damp so everything grows even if there's no rain. Estonia's pretty good in that sense. My feed's full of posts about burnt landscapes, destroyed rainforests, and all kinds of new and terrible records being broken. People dying of the heat, water shortages, famines, hurricanes. Everything's just getting more and more terrible. There are nights I can't sleep because the destruction makes me feel powerless and angry. The world's falling apart, it's overheating, and I can grow my potatoes here but what does that change? Around me life is broken, the system is flawed and wrong, and soon it will be too late to stop it all. I scroll through articles about climate anxiety that say you don't have to accept it, that you have to do something and help in some way, but even though I give money to protect the rainforests and nature and help refugees, why do I still feel like I'm trying to buy my way out of anxiety?

I know full well that anxiety doesn't help. Me losing sleep doesn't make the world any better. It's a nasty, vicious circle. I run my finger round a big mosquito bite, faster and faster, until I scrape the skin. It stings like hell.

Well, sweetie, how have you been? I'm still not hardened enough, hearing her say that makes something inside me feel warm. I know I can't get too soft. I need to hold on to my shell and protect myself. My mom's in a cheery mood and hugs me. She got here sooner than I expected. Bottles are clinking in the shopping bags.

I thought I'd come and help you a bit. There must be the odd thing that needs preparing? Where are we actually having the barbecue?

Mom's in full swing, she carries branches and old half-rotten planks to the campfire site and saws up a dried-out guelder rose bush. I like seeing her this way, but I know there'll be a setback tomorrow at the latest, maybe even tonight. That's how it is with holidays. As a child, I couldn't understand why my mom didn't like Christmas. Now I kind of do. After Dad left, Santa stopped visiting. The spruce branches went up inside and the lights were up, but there was no Christmas feeling. We sat vacantly at the table and gnawed blood sausage.

Mom wants to come and bustle around in the kitchen, but I say it's too small so it's better if she takes a breather. Or, if she really wants to, she can get some chives for the salad. There are lots of grill sausages in Mom's bag, and four bottles of wine: two white, two red. I put the white in the fridge. Good thing there's nothing stronger. Soon Tiina and Raivo will be here, and things will be more relaxed.

Mom and I sit outside drinking tea and then she gives me a funny look and asks, but can't you and

Tarmo still get back together? It'll be hard for you by yourself, she says, and that I can spend the summer here if I want, but in the fall, when I move back to town, I could still try and patch things up. Men aren't complicated in the least, she says. Make him something nice to eat and pour a couple of glasses of wine and then snuggle up, that'll do the trick.

This enrages me. It's over! I don't want him back!

But where are you going to live? my mom asks. How will you manage? After all, Tarmo has a good job and he's decent otherwise, doesn't drink, doesn't smoke. He's a good man. And smart too.

What would you know about that, Mom dear? I think, and I explode: How many times do I have to tell you, I don't want anyone, I just need to be by myself, don't you come lecturing me, you don't know anything at all!

Well, what is it I don't know? And it's not like you tell me anything, you don't talk to me at all.

The situation was simply that we weren't compatible anymore, do you understand?

Well I see that, but is there really nothing you could …

There are no buts! That's it, period.

You know you're not getting any younger, and soon maybe no one'll want you anymore. Sometimes it's better to have someone than to be alone. Things can be tough without a family of your own. And you can't put off having children forever, one day it'll be too late, you might regret it.

I'm already completely on edge and ready to leap up and go anywhere at all.

What are you getting so mad about? I don't mean it badly, why can't we have a conversation anymore? says

Mom, who probably doesn't realize she's crossed a line, who thinks all my choices in life are wrong and she would have done things much better. But didn't her facade collapse too?

Oh well. Look, I think we need more wood for the sauna, I'll go and get some.

I go to the stack and pile up an armful.

Well well, it's all quiet round here, I didn't know the soldiers got sent home for Midsummer too, says Raivo jokingly. He lives in Tallinn but comes from the south and the accent's still there. I don't know what these allied forces do—do they get a Midsummer bonfire too? Brits don't know anything about Midsummer; it's all foreign to them. You know though, if they do have one and start jumping over it, I want to see it with my own eyes. Hopping like little fleas.

I can't help rolling my eyes a little. Tiina takes over the conversation.

But don't they have that stone circle over in England, you know the one—you tell me, you're the clever one here Liine, what's it called, great big stones standing up.

Stonehenge.

Yeah, Stonehenge. That's got something to do with the equinox as well, hasn't it? So it's not all foreign to them.

Now Mom sticks her nose in. But still, they weren't the ones who built Stonehenge, it's so old, Brits today don't know the slightest thing about these old customs.

Not in the slightest, Raivo agrees.

But that way they'd get to know the local customs a bit, Tiina thinks. The bonfire and the sausages and …

And the beer! exclaims Raivo. Where'd that crate of beers go? Anyway, tell us what's new around here. Are they still shooting away like mad, or what?

Mom looks at me. Well, Liine would know most about that, she says. She's living here at the moment. This year we've got a summer resident.

Oh that's good, says Tiina, good to have someone staying here a bit longer, that'll stop it getting overgrown. I wish I could come out here more often, but looking after more than one place at the same time is too much. So what's it like living here all the time, Liine?

I shrug. Sometimes it's a bit much with the noise here, I say. But then some days it's all completely okay again. Sometimes when I go to the store, I can see boys in green crawling along the roadside ditches. You get kind of used to the guns firing, to the smaller shots, but not completely. They still scare me sometimes. And in the morning, they always start at the shooting range at eight on the dot.

Like a rooster, Raivo can't help adding. At least it makes you feel a bit safer, that if something kicks off, then the defending forces are nearby. Ukraine wouldn't have been able to put up any resistance if they didn't have soldiers there.

Easy for you to say, safe in the city, but if it comes to bombing, the first thing they target will be military objects like this, Mom butts in. And Liine, you don't even watch the news.

What would I watch it for? When the war starts I'll know about it without the news.

If your Mom calls, you still won't know, Raivo sniggers, you're already used to all the shooting.

My mouth stays firmly shut. I don't want to start explaining.

Well at least it's good that it's calmer at Midsummer, and people get some peace and quiet, Tiina sighs.

It's five in the morning and everyone's asleep. I pick up the plates, sausage packaging, and empty bottles lying around the fire. I'd like to shake the night away and pretend it's a normal day and that I'm not drowsy and tired and there aren't any drunk relatives asleep indoors. When I wake up, I want the traces of the night already gone, vanished.

All night I felt like a marionette, like Pinocchio, worrying that his nose might suddenly start growing, so I didn't say too much, just going mm-hm and well-well.

When the company was already in a merry state, but not yet too hazy, I asked about Elvi. What's the story, how did we get this house from her? I don't know anything about her. Tiina did most of the talking, and what I found out was this.

My grandma Vaike and her older sister Elvi grew up really near here, on a farm of which nothing remains. My great-grandfather Jaan had bought the place from the squire in Tsooru, who put up a lot of land for sale around here, and the peasants' bank granted loans on reasonable terms. The owners felled the trees, uprooted the stumps, and built houses with their own hands. That was how the whole village was built. People generally spent the first few years living in their saunas. Jaan married Ella and soon the children came along, five of them in total, but two boys died very young. That left two daughters, Vaike and Elvi, and one son, Peter, later a partisan who was killed in a bunker. Jaan was arrested for having been in the Home Guard militia during the German occupation, and most of his property was confiscated. Peter joined the Forest Brothers, as the partisans were known. Ella stayed with the girls and failed to meet the forestry requirements, after which Russians were allowed to settle on the farm and my great-grandmother fled. It was later said that the newcomers had stayed there for as long as there was anything to take, the outbuildings were chopped up for firewood, and everything soon fell apart. For a few years they hid themselves and lived wherever they could. Vaike was with relatives in Antsla, Elvi somewhere near Sõmerpalu, and their mother moved around from place to place. After a few years, an opportunity arose to go and live in Võru. It felt safer in the town, but they were still afraid of persecution.

Vaike got married in the fifties and went to live in Tartu, but Elvi was a spinster and didn't want to live in a town. Although she had suitors, she never got involved with anyone and never married. Elvi lived the whole of her adult life in Võru and worked in the library, but as she got older—this was in the mid-seventies— she began to reconnect with people from her home region. Selma was on her own in Tsõriksoo after her husband died, and Elvi began coming to help her out. When Selma died, she left the farm to Elvi, who lived and worked here for the rest of her life.

A lot of this story was new to me. I didn't know my roots were near here. Neither Grandma nor Mom had talked about it, although Grandma wasn't in the habit of talking about herself much anyway.

It explains why this landscape feels so familiar.

One day I should go and look for the ruins of my grandma's childhood home.

The morning is painful. Mom's up early, making pancakes. The rooms don't have doors, only curtains pulled in front of the doorways, with a greasy smell seeping through them. And sounds. They're discussing percentages, and I don't know whether it's interest rates or something else. My head's heavy and spinning.

I wander into the kitchen and pour myself some coffee. As I enter, the tone of the conversation changes. But maybe I'm just imagining it.

Aunt Tiina starts talking about grave sites, saying she still needs to visit the cemetery before they go back to town, and then they have a lengthy discussion about what and where and how, because everyone's buried somewhere different. The conversation goes in one ear and out the other as I eat too-greasy pancakes with jam. Behind the window the crow swings on the branches of the pear tree.

You ought to do a bit more around here. I don't immediately understand that it's aimed at me, and I look up, bewildered. I was lost in my own safe, empty world, secluded and quiet. Raivo points at the meadow, to where the cow parsley is gleaming. Those need cutting back, he says. I'd rather not say just how goddamn much I've done already this year. Do you want to help me? I respond. I should have brought a trimmer, he sighs. Yeah, well, there's a scythe. That works too, he laughs, if you haven't got anything better to do. I shrug my shoulders. It probably won't take any longer with the scythe.

Mom starts a monolog, at first as if defending me, saying Liine's done a nice job here, but then she falls back into reproaches. She talks as if she's been here with me all this time holding my hand, as if it's only because of her I've done anything: she's the one who taught me to hold an ax, to draw water from a well, as if I can't cope without her at all. After all, Liine calls her mom to ask how to make a bed and where to empty the dry toilet—Liine, who shouldn't have gone off to study Estonian philology, because look at her now, sitting here hunched over her texts not making any money. She wraps me up inside her words until I want to start screaming. Liine, who ought to have a slightly better idea of what she's doing, Liine, who doesn't even have a man anymore. She talks faster and faster, as if I wasn't there.

My throat's constricted. I get up, grab the empty buckets from the corner and go and fetch some water.

A puff of warm wind. I turn the pump. Cold water. I splash water on my face and swear quietly.

When I come back, Mom's tone has softened. She's stacked up the dirty dishes, and she says, in a voice that seems learned from a soap opera: Everything's going great, isn't it? I don't know what's great exactly, but I know it's best to say nothing.

They're gone. At last. Mom had to wait until nightfall before she was ready to drive. I'm tired. I can breathe out again and I can shake my body, but the tension isn't fading. Some feelings come back: some discomfort, from somewhere deep inside, restlessness and heaviness. I'm on my own again, floating in this great sea where there are no shores. Hot, rancid air. I'm soaked, my skin is salty. Relief, emptiness, anger. I'd like to kill someone, but I don't have anyone but me. All the knives are rusty and blunt anyway.

I'd been wearing an old outfit for the family visit, one I hadn't worn in a long time and I don't like wearing in the slightest, one that squeezes and rubs against me and makes me itch. I don't want a clown's smile on my face anymore, but I don't dare remove it either. It's easier to look like a good daughter for a few days a year.

I've been hiding in myself all my life, because once you've learned to keep your distance and be far-off and unreachable, it becomes a comfortable smoke-screen to float behind. Show yourself and your imperfection seems too scary.

It's raining at last. Heavy droplets fall, their strong fists striking the ground, the petals, the roof, my face. I run to get the towel from the line, throw it onto the chair indoors, and go to the doorway to look at the rain. It's thundering and suddenly the sky blazes white. The thunder is pretty close. A thirsty earth greedy for water, and I gulp for air like an amphibian on dry land for the first time.

It rains all the following day. With clear intervals, but I can't get anything done outside. I'm sitting at the kitchen table trying to do some work but I can't really concentrate. I still find myself staring vacantly out the window. I look at the oak I climbed as a child, and the rosehip bush, which spreads out right next to it without even bothering to bloom. The beautiful bluish-purple flowers of the irises are right beside them: the rain hasn't beaten them down. I keep the kitchen door open. The sound of rain is pleasant and the air is fresh, invigorating. Eventually my toes start getting cold.

I'm like an unknown continent where everything already exists and where the paths have long been trampled on. But the explorers who arrived by ship have given the rivers and lakes and mountains names that are unsuited to them; they've infected me with their language, they've colonized me. I need to go back to my beginnings and I need to rediscover my own eyes and purge myself of your judgments. Purge myself of Mom. I feel like a child left alone at home, forgotten in a ghostly apartment, thrown into the body of an adult without the ability to cope with life. I look like an adult, but there's a child inside who's upset, frightened and hesitant.

I can handle myself. I could when I was a kid, why would I not be able to now? I can handle things. I'll find a way to see myself with compassion and find the right questions. What do I need? A change. Something has changed, something is slightly different.

Seized by some strange compulsion, I'm rummaging through the top drawer of the dresser again, the one with the papers. This time I'm not looking for light bulbs or anything like that. Instead, I want confirmation of what Tiina said. I don't even know what that might be. What do I want to know? What do I want to prove? Before I heard the story from Tiina, I had this crazy idea that maybe Elvi was a lesbian. Weren't old spinsters and bachelors often secretly gay? That would be so wonderful. Maybe she and Selma were a couple. One sixty, the other nearly eighty. Is there a love story here? What does a typical love story even look like? An older man hooks up with a woman fifteen years younger, one who's just turned eighteen? Excuse me while I laugh.

Elvi never married. Selma had been married but had no children. How does it even happen that you start helping an older person and then you move in, and then they leave the house to you in a will? It makes me think of those stories about unfortunate old people who've signed their property over to someone and then get evicted from their homes. Elvi and Selma lived together for a long time, about ten years. It was mutually beneficial, and at that time small houses in the country barely cost anything. In fact, people just wanted to get rid of the miserable rotting piles that reminded them of their origins, the numerous outbuildings requiring maintenance and repair. Forget poverty and slaving from dawn to dusk, forget old-fashioned rooms with earthen floors, swap it all for a desk in an office and a centrally heated apartment, mock the folly of your ancestors who didn't know how to enjoy life. No, there was nothing romantic about the countryside—only poverty and hard work.

It's odd to think about how mechanically lives pass by. I can no longer understand how I was able to spend so many years with a person who treated me like a commodity. Who saw me as a kind of mineral deposit that he could extract energy from, no matter how dark and raw it might be at times. I'm beginning to understand your anger: if the profits stop coming, if the other's resisting and no longer allowing the exploitation, then this will lead to anger. You were like my mom, except you were even crueler. My body no longer belonged to me: you were keeping a record and my consent wasn't worth asking for. I gave away my body, or even shoved it into your arms like some rotten, brittle thing I was tired of, a burden. Something for everyone except me to do things to. And now I'm reclaiming myself. It's a vulnerable feeling. The scent of carrion rises into my nose. But what is it that's rotting—me, or what I decided to leave?

The rain did everything good. No more feeling like everything's burning up, and now it's all greener and cooler. The end of June and the berries on the bushes are almost ripe. It's weird they're so early. Everything's happening faster than I remembered, in a rush, in a spurt, like it wants to get somewhere. And the place I've come to, this place I've put myself in, oscillates along with me, everything I do and everything I don't do immediately leaves a mark. Sometimes the land is for me and sometimes it turns against me, closing around me in a demanding manner. It's not me, it's the land itself: it's steering me, it's dragging me somewhere, and it's not moving in one straight line. It's crisscrossing to and fro.

Strange thoughts like these cross my mind sometimes.

The currants are still a bit unripe, but you can pick the odd one here and there and eat them in your porridge. While weeding under the bushes I taste the gooseberries. They're hard: they really are unripe. When I was little, my sister and I always ate the bushes half-empty before the berries were properly ripe. The sour crunch between your teeth is like jumping head-first into water, into a familiar lake, into transparent depths. I need to remember those moments too, full of warming sunshine, light and friendship.

I'd like to write to Pille, ask her how things are going.

I'd like not to be worried she'll give me a one-word answer: fine.

I'd like to be glowing, I'd like to swing in the wind and fly around, scattering like seed.

You told me I don't even know how to love. I don't believe that anymore. Maybe I didn't know how to love you, and I cowered at your words and hid myself. I tried to please you, but I was afraid of you. In the end, all I showed you was a surface; I learned to reflect you.

Even though I know you wanted to hurt me, you've still succeeded in sowing doubt in me. That was your strength.

The spot I dug up here the first day is now a vegetable patch. The first rucola and dill plants have come up, and beet leaves too. I do some weeding and think about how I like to do my best to take care of the plants. I like to look at them, talk to them, weed them, water them in the evenings. If I can love these little plants poking their heads out of the ground, if I can love the big oak tree that's been full of beautiful young green leaves all this time, and the peonies that bloom so sweetly, if I can love cold well water and birds and a fox with a raggedy tail and the white sea of cow parsley, then I can love everything else.

The body is a never-ending battleground. The glasses have been rattling again since the morning. I'm sitting at the table trying to proofread but the table's shaking. The vibration spreads to my fingers, arms and shoulders; my whole body. It drives me crazy, even if there's Balkan postpunk playing on my headphones and I keep telling myself the war is far away. The war is not far away; only five hundred meters from here. Simulations, maneuvers, war games. Won't the land be blown up here, won't animals flee, won't birds be frightened all the same?

I can't help thinking that there's a war going on inside me. This war might begin fairly mildly, with some slight remarks about appearance, a joke with a sexual undertone, the default assumption that women are worse than men at so many things. And at the other end of the scale: rape, abuse, violence. Rape is a war crime. But there's not much sense in going to court in peacetime because you might not have put up enough resistance. Laws are made by men; they protect men.

I remember one time when I was a schoolgirl I took the bus to my mom's job. It was late springtime, I was lightly dressed and was wearing a red fake leather jacket that was open at the front. I might have been twelve. I sat by the window and a young man, maybe twenty, sat down next to me. Tall, dark-haired. After a while, I felt him pressing against me, and I shifted closer to the window. Soon he was clinging to me again. I tried to make myself as small as possible, but there was nowhere else to go as the window was in the way. I was trapped. I crossed my leg over my knee, his legs spread wider and wider. Suddenly he grabbed my chest. Grabbed my still-budding left breast. I pushed his hand away and got up, I don't remember if I had to ask him to let me pass. I went to the other end of the bus with my heart pounding. I got off at the next stop. Then, to my horror, I realized he was following me. I looped back, went to a market where there were a lot of people, and lost sight of him. Just as I thought I'd shaken him off, he walked along the street toward me. He tried to stop me, shouting something, but I was already running, running like a streak of lightning. Maybe he wanted to apologize. But maybe he wanted something else. My twelve-year-old self did what she could and fled.

I switch off the laptop. Can't work here today. I drive for half an hour and sit in a café at the foot of Munamägi Hill to calm down and just be. I order a large coffee, put on my headphones, and hope the war will be over by the evening.

maybe you should just stop talking to her, Silja says in Messenger.

your mom is toxic and you know it and you can't actually change anything

true, and I've been thinking about it too but it feels so hard, like she's the reason I even exist - how do I cut her out of my life?

seriously... who took care of you when you were a kid? your mom put you in the role of an adult and you had to take care of her AND your sister when you were like ten or something

eight actually

yep so I'd wonder whether it's wise keeping her in your life. does she give you anything or only take?

give? I don't know what she gives me besides guilt. though she can sometimes be nice when she's in a good mood. of course you can't compare with your mom. you still seem to have a perfectly good relationship

we're okay. not mega close but we get along pretty well and talk to each other

well you went on a trip together and spend time together like normal people. you're not drained of energy after spending time with her, right?

nope not really

well you're very lucky. and I have to just work with the material I have. at least she's there in some form

it's hard to cut off your mom of course. but people do it when there's a reason. I've heard of it happening. you're an adult just like her and you can make your own choices even if it means ending a relationship.

maybe you're having a major clear-out in your life right now where you have to look at what to get rid of and what to keep

I don't know I feel like I still owe her something

what??

that's the weird guilt I can't explain... like I don't want to spend time with her but I can still pick up the phone. like on a kind of minimal level

and your sister, does she talk to your mom?

even less than me, as far as I know

mmm well adults can generally take care of themselves

not my mom. she needs people around her

to overwhelm them with her problems...

possibly. I dunno but it seems really hardcore just to block someone. like how I do it at all. "dear mom I don't want to talk to you anymore now. please don't call, don't write, don't contact me"

you don't have to say anything, just don't answer anymore. like you did with tarmo

god I can't even imagine what kind of accusations would follow, maybe that's the point? that no one should have to put up with this kind of bullshit, but it still feels kind of scary

Things feel uncertain now and then.

Some days are a bit better, but sometimes I don't know if I can trust anyone anymore. Or even trust time itself and that everything can gradually get better.

I've slept so badly for several nights that I feel like I'm about to shatter, like my body's weighed down and my head is blurry. Coffee doesn't help but the day needs to be gotten through somehow.

I'm thinking about you less and less. Our relationship was like a bad book that ended. I finally put it down, but only after reading it from cover to cover out of some strange sense of duty, and then realizing it wasn't meant for me. Or maybe it was, and I still haven't figured it out. I don't know.

On days like this, I watch time pass with a strange detachment, as if I were someone else. It's distance and presence at once: the seconds become visible, linearity disappears, and all times exist at once. It's Selma and Elvi's time, it's my time, there's time yet to come, wild and vastly incomprehensible. But in this wilderness there is some clarity, some brightness.

A shadow cut from the same cloth as me has followed me, walked in my steps with love, and sent me relationships. I've put up with more than I should. I believed that I was in the wrong, and that was why my parents were unable to love me. I've refused to see how I was abandoned and I've been dismissive of my wounds. I've excused violence with love, linking the two together. But I have to separate them. Violence doesn't love; violence owns.

I'm picking currants. The bigger bushes here are taller than me, I need to get inside them to get berries from the middle branches. It smells so good here. It's the smell of summer, the smell of being alive. But the ants have become my enemies: if I see them wandering around anywhere, I immediately spot the curled-up leaves with aphid eggs underneath them. I break off the shoots and throw them into the fireplace to light a fire later. I fetch the saw to prune the lower, dried-out branches. The berries are large and soft and their dark bodies are close to bursting between my fingers. I circle around the bushes with a bucket, slowly, like the sun. The clouds are gathering again: the thick white pillows have turned an ominous gray. When one of the bushes is empty, I want to burn off the pests straight away. I light a bonfire that gives off thick smoke because the branches are young and the leaves are green. But the fire finally starts, the leaves shrink, the branches crackle.

The wind rises and the aspens come to life. Their leaves sway and flicker, and everything around me moves and breathes. In about twenty seconds, the drizzle turns into a heavy rainstorm so I have to run indoors. I sit on a small bench in the doorway and look at the garden from behind the mosquito net. How many times have I sat here watching the rain like this? I don't even want to boil water for tea, because the kettle's old and hums too loudly.

I'm starting to miss people. Eye contact, conversation, company. Here sometimes I don't feel like I'm a person: I'm air, I'm a leaf, I'm a sweet pea twisting around the cane. Yet at the same time I'm afraid of being out among people. I want to hide between the leaves, wrap them around me like a blanket, like the aphids do in the blackcurrant bushes. I'm still too vulnerable and I don't want it to show. I'm building a new shell, but how long will it take? I'm crackling, I'm expanding, and I'm afraid of getting hurt. I'm afraid of getting stepped on. Yet I still miss closeness. I'm scared, and missing people. That's just how it is.

The days have begun to pass quickly. Time that once stretched out sweetly like endless pink chewing-gum has changed and is starting to pulsate faster. There's a peacefulness in my movements and thoughts, but I can't shake off the feeling that it's temporary. I push away any thoughts about the end of summer or about having to go back to another life, to other rules, to the city where decisions have to be made and where people outnumber trees.

Summer is ripe and lush. The yarrow's flowering by the pond and small frogs jump around in the grass after it rains. Sometimes I go to the library in Tsooru. The library's mostly closed in the summer, but every two weeks it opens and then heaps of people visit it. Mostly older ladies, of course, who stay to chat for a while, and sometimes a local gentleman with anecdotes he needs to share. I borrow old twentieth-century novels, and new slender books in translation from Looming Press—for the first time in ages I feel how nice it is to get lost in fiction again. The last time I was reading like this was when I was a teenager, when I was fourteen, fifteen, eighteen … In the evening I read on the couch and in the morning at the kitchen table. Sometimes in the shade of the oak tree, at least as long as no insects come and bother me. The wasps have appeared. Another sign that summer won't last.

I'm lounging around in the garden when I get a strange message from a girl I know on Messenger. She asks how I'm doing and if everything's going fine.

yes, spending summer in the countryside. how about you?

fine. saw tarmo yesterday and he told me something weird

about what?

well, he'd been drinking and pretty heavily. it was late too. but if you're fine then it's probably nothing

what did he say?

something about you were gone, and that you were having some kind of depressive period

ok no that's bullshit. we broke up and I'm in the countryside. but he's the depressive one

mm yeah seemed that way but then he seemed really interested in it and asked had I seen you and are you with someone

wtf is it to him

well he talked about it for a long time. something about orgies and how women are even quicker at getting their panties off than men … well you can probably imagine, it was the kind of crap drunks come out with, annoying and stupid. but since I haven't seen you in a long time I thought I'd check up on you

really. he is absolutely unbelievable

well, at least you know what's going on. good you're doing fine

I'm doing fine, yeah. totally chilling in the country. but don't tell him anything about me. seriously don't

ok. but you know he just seemed v sad

sad my ass. he's a psycho. what fucking orgies?!

that was ott, right? hey but have fun in the country

Laundry day. Towels and shirts flapping in the wind. The sun shining again as if it had never rained. The air's suffocatingly hot; soon there will be more thunder. The morning was really quiet for a good while, with no noise from the shooting range. The silence gave me the strength to do the laundry. There's no washing machine.

Yesterday's conversation irritated me. I don't want to know what you're saying about me in town or how you're badmouthing me. What a sneaky, petty way of getting at me. I bet you knew that girl would pass it all on to me. Where did the sad guy who's worried about his ex's fucking panties come from? How magnanimous of you to be concerned! My anger's back: it's rigid and sharp. I curse out loud. I'd like to beat up the laundry, not that my shirts and underwear deserve it, but I remember reading somewhere about how they used to beat the dirt out with sticks.

I look at my hands. The washing powder has dried them and they've become rough. The skin on my palms is flaking and the callouses are getting thicker. And I don't know if it's just that it looks that way, but more lines seem to have appeared. Crisscrossing my palms. The backs of my hands are burned from the sun.

I've lost my fake straw hat from the fast fashion chain. But the sun's too ferocious to go without it. I remember the headscarves I saw in the big closet. That could work, a scarf would fit in nicely here. I go inside and rummage around in the closet—there are plenty of scarves here, just choose what kind of vibe you want. This is how people used to do things. There are brown, yellow and green ones. Scarves made of proper thick fabric, several nylon ones. My hand digs deeper until it touches a package behind a heap of towels—a bag made of thick plastic. Without much thought, I pull it out. A packet of letters! I open it curiously, with no hesitation. I was beginning to think the dead weren't talking and that was how things would remain.

The first thing my finger lands on is a photo of a woman wearing pince-nez. The photo's slightly faded; the light falls from the left, leaving the right side of her face almost completely in shadow. She has short hair, she's somewhere in her thirties, and her expression is self-assured. She wears a dark, loose-fitting blouse with a collar. She looks smart and fairly educated. Might be a teacher or an official. On the back it says *carte postale* and is stamped: Auksmann at 2 Riga Street in Tartu. Who's it a photo of? I don't recognize her, but how would I know what Elvi looked like when she was young? Oh, hold on, it's more likely to be Selma, because the stamp seems to be from Estonia's first period of independence before the war.

I unfold the first letter. It's written on lined paper in old-fashioned handwriting with no addressee.

December 4, 1951

Hello my darling!

I was supposed to write to you as soon as I got home. But the thing is there's so little time that somehow it never works out. I work terribly fast every day. Between yesterday and today we processed 10 cubic meters of wood! I'm deadly tired of logging right now! You can already tell from this letter that my hand is used to holding an ax handle but not a pen. But nothing's wrong! I'd rather put my head in your lap right now, and then I'd feel truly at rest. But dreams are just dreams, they don't come true!

Maybe you're wondering when I'm coming to Võru. If not before the holidays, then definitely after. There's no obstacle I can think of that could stop me. All I need is willpower, and that's what I have. I'd like to see you, just the thought of it makes me happy. You might not believe it, because I never show you whether I'm happy or sad. You have my words and my letter to prove it, and right now I'm a bit sad that I can't be with you and talk about everything. But that time will come again.

In the meantime, I suggest you spend the holidays having some fun. And then have a good rest—do you never feel tired?

Once again,
  Happy Holidays,
  Selma

Selma's handwriting is a little rounded but legible. The bottom of the paper's slightly torn. The letters are well preserved, considering more than seventy years have passed. They've been kept and re-read; they've lived longer than some people do. Blue ink on beige paper, straight lines and exclamations. Did Selma post this letter from here? There's no indication. It could have been sent from anywhere. If you believe Aunt Tiina, Selma didn't move here until the sixties. And who's the addressee?

The laundry's outside and the water has definitely cooled down by now and I don't care.

My hand holds the ax handle, my hand holds the knife.

I open one letter after another.

June 7, 1951

Elvi, beloved!

I have a yearning in my heart for you. My legs are worn out from walking to and from the mailbox. Even back on 1 June (!), I went down to the mailbox several times a day—but there was no letter from you, what a disappointment!

Your first letter only arrived on Sunday night, the second one tonight and that's it.

Seriously darling (and here's a kiss), I miss you. You know, I haven't looked at other girls at all, they don't attract me, and if one of them did, then I'd close my eyes or turn my head away. Is that what you do?

I'm glad you're doing well, just don't stay indoors all the time. Take a book with you and get some sun. My skin has already picked up some color, and then you can't be a swan either.

What have I been doing? I eat well, sleep badly(!) and work diligently.

However, last night I went to the cinema—Papa, Mama, the Maid and I. Interesting film, you ought to watch it. A French film, full of kissing.

We've had warm and sunny weather all this time, it was only today that things went awry and it rained. Until then it was marvelous weather, I went around in just a jacket not even thinking about diphtheritic angina at all.

By the way, both the Bus Station and Gloria have put up their prices, vodka (that good drink) by 75% and wine by 50%. What a blow! Now how will they keep the masses of the amusement-seeking human race from falling on the Beach Café like an avalanche—poor old wooden house, it is being danced to bits!

Sleep well, dream about me sometimes, and I'll kiss and hug you really tight right now.

Kisses, Leo

Who the hell is Leo? The package contains a handful of letters from different points in time and in different handwriting, and some photos. There's a very small photo of an older woman sitting on some steps, a white cat beside her. The picture was taken just as the cat jumped down the steps, so it's turned into a long white waterfall with paws. She's wearing a white dress and glasses—it's the same woman who was photographed at Auksmann's. She's looking down at the cat, and next to her there's a tall flowering bush. It's a summery, bright photo. She looks around forty or fifty, sitting on her hands like she doesn't know what to do with them, or feels a little awkward in front of the photographer.

There's also a picture from a funeral with a group of strangers standing together—the children looking at the photographer, the old men looking at each other or to the side, and some women looking at the mound. There are lots of flowers, and *Helmut* is written on the back of the photo in red ink. I don't see the woman with glasses, unless she's one of the old women in headscarves in the front row. From the clothes, it looks like it could be the 1970s. Pine tree trunks tower behind the mourners. It's as if the cemetery's inside a bush. There are alder shoots right next to the wreaths. It's strange.

And then there's a postcard full of *reminders to self* in messy handwriting. Clearly copied from somewhere.

1. Always stand by your words and demands. Defend your opinions if you know you are right. 2. Don't compare yourself with others. Enjoy what you have. No one can be perfect. Don't torment yourself trying to achieve what you're not capable of. 3. Be kind to yourself. 4. Always finish what you decide to start, and you will be taken seriously. 5. Wear clothes that you feel comfortable in. You could dress as if you were going to meet ...

And here it breaks off, I can't make out the next word. With the director? With the doctor? Neither is right, but some important person apparently ... That way you will look good in any situation and feel confident.

The Eesti Raamat postcard has blueweed on it and long green plants with white flowers against a black background. These recommendations aren't bad at all. Be kind to yourself, I repeat to myself, be kind to yourself, then there will be hope of retaining some sanity in this mad world.

I don't manage to read the whole package. I go to bed that evening with swirly handwriting jumping around in front of my eyes. I'd like to understand Elvi and Selma better. I'd like to know their story.

I need to run away. Not from you now, and not from Mom either. I need to run away from myself. And from this place. You might call it a longing for people and different surroundings. I need to go into town. I need to talk. I'm tired of myself. Being alone in the countryside turns you a little strange. Like the neighbor who came to bring me cucumbers on Saturday morning, a bottle of vodka in his back pocket. A tiny man, well past forty, with deep lines on his face. He appeared suddenly and silently; there he was in the garden. It turned out that he's lived here for six years, after a long time working as a builder in Finland, where he earned enough money to live quietly for a good while. I offered him some coffee but luckily he didn't come inside. He just said, Look, I've got a cucumber glut here, and he asked if I was by myself. He promised he could always help if anything needed doing. I thanked him—you never know when a tree might fall or your car might break down. And then he went back home, leaving a plastic bag of cucumbers by the well.

My skin is tanned and a little dry, while my hands have become more veined. Eyes scrunched up, my body carrying strange burdens of feelings: sometimes light, sometimes as heavy as lead. I breathe deeply, like a person who wants to be alive and dead at the same time, like someone who's forgotten how to breathe and is now learning it again. My lungs are working; air comes like a relief, like life, like a gentle reminder that this lightness can burn, flames can burst from inside, and that it's possible to hurt yourself. And so, in the meantime, I find myself back in the city, in a small cafe on the corner, where I gaze at the cute windows of old wooden houses and the people walking by. I find a look in a friend's eyes that reflects my humanity, and a party where I dance and forget myself. Maybe I'll be ready to move back here soon.

It's still sultry in the morning, the weather forecast doesn't promise anything good.

Mom's name flashes on my phone. I look at it steadily. Accept or decline? In the end I give in.

Liine, do you even know there's a storm coming?

I heard the news, yes, there's going to be a heavy storm.

Not just a heavy storm, but a superstorm. Are you sure you're going to stay in the countryside? Couldn't you go back into town?

I've just been to town! What's better in town?

It's safer! There are people around, after all.

Mom, listen, there's people around here, too.

How can there be, you're all by yourself, for god's sake!

The neighbors are all home. And I can handle it.

What will you do if there's a power cut?

What I always do. I have candles, matches, I can cook on the stove. I'll survive. I've seen a storm before.

I don't know what sort of summer this is, it's always raining and impossible to go to the coast at all, and then there's storms like this one.

This is climate change.

But what sort of global warming is it when it's cold and rainy? I'd really like some warmth in the summer too so I can still get a tan.

It's 40 Celsius everywhere in southern Europe right now. We're lucky here, to be honest.

I don't want that much heat you know, 25 or so would do, but not more than 30. Of course this would have to happen just when I'm on vacation. I still had some annual leave left from last year, but how do you know when the weather will be nice? You can't be sure of anything at all, we don't get normal warm weather in July these days. First you water the garden like crazy. You know, I've completely done myself in with this watering, I can feel it in my back. I guess I should go to the doctor. I feel like there's something wrong with the discs in my spine, the same thing your grandma had. But I don't want an operation. And the next thing you know, it's all cold and wet, and no chance of any beach weather. I don't think I'll get a tan this year.

This is the Estonian dream: warm, but not hot, rain, but not too much, right?

Well, I don't know what that's supposed to mean. I just wanted to check you know there's going to be a big storm, and hail too apparently, so that you're prepared. You don't watch the news or anything.

I find out about things too.

There's also been those hailstones as big as a fist, smashing up car windscreens and greenhouses. You cover up the car windows, else there'll be cracks. Then you'll come crying.

I'll deal with it, don't worry.

And put everything in the yard inside so it can't fly away. The wind's going to be very strong.

I stored away everything in the yard this morning. *You* make sure you don't fly away.

Me? I'm not flying anywhere.

The wind really picks up by the afternoon, blowing like crazy. It's as if it wants to sweep everything out of its way. Twigs fall from the trees and the plants twist as if dancing. But it's not a joyful dance; it's a surrender to the wind's fury, as if it spoke with your voice and was giving an order: Dance! And you have to dance out of fear. Somewhere a tree crashes. I go back inside and find the power's gone. There's no phone signal either. For a moment it's scary. What if something does happen? But then I remember the man next door and relax a bit. And really, what could happen? If it gets too scary, I can call on the neighbors. They wouldn't mind—quite the opposite.

I sit on the green couch by the window and see the treetops tossing about as the forest sways. The wind has pushed the younger apple trees down. Crashing; flashes of light: the thunder is pretty close. I wonder how much storm damage there will be, and how long it will take for the power to come back on. And I pick up the letters again.

October 15, 1957

Dearest Elvi!

Thank you very much for the long letter.

Now I know all the happy and sad news from where you are.

You're a young person and you have a profession of your own—you can be your own mistress and do what you want. You won't have a wedding, but it's probably for the best that your marriage wasn't yet registered, because it's hardly likely that anything good would have come from living with Leo.

That Aimee bagged another woman's man very easily. But you can be sure that something like this would have happened sooner or later. There's no point in waiting for Leo to come to his senses. At the same time, it's not wise to start looking for another suitor straight away.

You need to get to know the other person better first, so as not to be disappointed again.

In the evening we watch the television at Johanna's. My aunt was here too. She's in Pechory right now. She'll be back soon. Maybe her hard life has made her nervous.

We all went down with the 'flu. Shop assistants are covering up their mouths and noses. The schools haven't been closed, but a lot of people are sick.

Lea's still living with her husband, with greater tolerance these days than in the beginning.

I'm still half sick. The 'flu hasn't completely left me yet.

Otherwise, things are all as they used to be.

It was lovely to see those pictures of you. Write to me and tell me about your life. Your letter made me happy.

Wishing you all the best,
    Auntie Hilda

In the evening, when the big storm's over and I go to bed in the pitch dark, I'm still thinking about this letter to Elvi, written by her aunt, trying to comfort and advise her at the same time. Elvi must have had a life of her own, that's for sure. And things turned out badly with Leo as well. Maybe that's why she never got married. Who knows if she found someone else after that? People can be disappointed once and for all, lose all confidence and withdraw into a cocoon. She must have been over thirty at the time she received this letter from her aunt. In the fifties I think she'd already have been considered an old maid. What else was there to do, but start knitting a sock and watch TV in the evenings? I'm thinking about what my mom said to me; soon no one would want me anymore. Where do these phrases come from? Is this something Mom was told, too, and Elvi before her?

And then I think about the photo of the two women. One of them's Elvi, the one with the glasses. The woman next to her is a little younger, with dark hair and a beautiful long nose. She looks at the camera, Elvi looks at her and smiles to herself—not a smile put on for a photographer, but the joy of company, the presence of this woman. The background is dark, but you can tell they're sitting at a table. This picture is almost shockingly intimate; it's obvious how free they feel and how close their friendship is. Elvi's wearing a colored blouse. I don't know what shade it might have been, maybe something bright. Was this picture taken before or after the engagement fell through?

When I'm in photographs, I'm on edge, tense, and I look awkward, like someone's trying to attack me. But I don't see myself from the sidelines when I'm really happy. Those moments exist too.

But there are the other moments. I don't actually know if I'm more hurt by my own imperfections or those of the world. When I'm outside lying on a thick rag rug and looking at the blades of grass, things don't seem all that terrible. But then there's the sound of a gunshot that brings me back to a reality where everything's dying. Ahead lies our good old Anthropocene highway. I don't know how to deal with destruction. Dying itself wouldn't be hard, because it wouldn't change anything. But I've learned to see the beauty around me, and the thought of it disappearing seems terrible.

In the morning, I rake and clean the yard because there are twigs all over the place. Larger branches I take to the firepit. On the far side of the yard, an aspen's fallen that could heat this whole place. The power will be back on in the afternoon. I read in the news that the storm tore the roof off an apartment building ten kilometers away, and a lot of trees have been damaged around the store in Tsooru. The roads are being cleared. Fortunately I don't need to go anywhere. The air is fresh, no longer sultry, but the sky is still gray and threatening.

In the garden I wash the dishes and wonder what kind of life these women had here together. Did they manage to create a life they were really happy with, despite the depressing times they lived in? Tsõriksoo is simply not a place that everyone understands. It has a power of its own, and if you stay here long enough, you'll learn to function within it, even love it. You may curse the cow parsley and the nettles, but if you throw a bag of potatoes into the soil in spring, they'll give you a decent harvest even when there's a drought.

You can feel the power of women here. Aunt Tiina said there was a farmer living here a hundred years ago, but he didn't last very long. This farm was run by women. The knowledge gives me strength, because if women were running this place alone in the past, then so can I. And I have other ways to earn my living besides this place. I wonder if they found a kind of freedom here. And the women before them? There were two sisters who lived here before Selma.

I want to be free, as free as Selma and Elvi are in my

imagination, but like them, I don't want to be alone. I want to break those molds that I've been pushed into and am used to moving within. Now my being swells quietly, seeking a form of its own. Taking up more and more space, and no longer caring about pleasing people. Tsõriksoo has helped break down boundaries and the frozen situations that I've been in, and that's strange, but nice. Maybe the enchantment will disappear when I leave here, but something's at work inside me that won't truly disappear. There could always be a relapse, but then I can just return for a moment, even just in my mind, and simply be here again and feel this way. I want to be brave. I don't want to be afraid anymore. I want to be free. I want life to flow through me. I want to be the current and the riverbed, the air and the droplets of water that shine brightly as they rush over the rocks.

I'm starting to dream. To dream of how I would like to live, and, what's more, what kind of family I'd like to have. These are jumpy thoughts, impulses: more about textures and smells and colors than solid outlines. I'd like to know more about plants. I want to have good friends by my side. I want to move and dance and feel joy. I want to move along the cut line, run through my fears and hesitations—my body's the blade that will cut them open. I've been living in a narrow box that pressed in from all sides. How used I was to this box, how well I knew these walls, how quickly I embraced its restrictions and character. But now a different room is emerging: one where there's space, where there's hope that things can be different, and that it really is possible to create something. Not only should negative patterns be broken; they must be crushed. With full force. Blocks have to be smashed to pieces. I'm still full of uncertainty because I don't know if I can trust myself completely. When I look at myself, I see contradictions and traumas and I see how everything I want to let go of has made me who I am. Is that still true though?

Maybe these dreams aren't determined by fate as much as I thought. Elvi clearly also tried to love in the traditional way: to find a man who'd hold her, get married, have children, build a house ... but then the wedding didn't happen. I'd love to know what Elvi wrote in her letters. What she felt, what she complained about, what she rejoiced over.

But I know she was ready to make a big change at the age of sixty, and move out of town. And that there were women in her life: there were friends, there were aunts. And Selma, who was old enough to be her mother. I'd like to believe that she was truly happy at last in Tsõriksoo, sitting right in front of the house looking up at the beautiful young crown of this same oak tree. Moving among the flowerbeds, carrying water, standing tall, finally breathing fully and deeply.

September 22, 1980

Dearest!

Yesterday your letter arrived saying you'd be here soon. I wait for you every day! Of course I understand that you won't show up at any other time than Sunday, and I don't know whether your day off is still Monday or a different day now.

I'm busy putting away the potato harvest, sorting the potatoes. I've done two of the boxes, but I still need to fill up the third. The new potatoes need to be kept separate from the seed potatoes.

So I'll wait! I can't even go to Helmut's grave because how would I know if you were arriving just then.

Yesterday the supports were put up on the cellar ceiling. The neighbor helped. The chimney was repaired yesterday too, it's marvelous not having rainwater coming through the ceiling anymore.

Everyone around here's harvesting potatoes. I'm the only one digging up the spuds on my own. Every day I dig up a few and take them away by cart.

So I'll wait! Impatiently!

See you soon, with pleasure!

Selma

I read this letter, the most recent one of them all. Maybe there was a wonderful fall with wonderful times ahead, forty-five years ago. It's nice to have a friend to wait for. I don't know if Elvi actually came to visit. But I guess she did.

The light is bright and pierces my skull before I've even properly opened my eyes. I'm alone in bed, but I'm still trying to wrap myself in an empty duvet cover and hide myself, so the day can't find me. The air is damp and suffocating. I'd like to carry on sleeping, but there's no hope of that. It's morning and there's a whole day ahead and at least half my life, and I don't want to start dealing with any of it.

I cry all morning. This hasn't happened to me in months. Now it seems like something from my old life is back. My insides are cramped; some feelings want to get out, but I can't name them. And so I have to become those feelings. It was stupid of me to think that my constant sadness was bound up with you and that if I left, I'd be rid of it all. This cruel depression. I'm so fragile that the sound of gunshots from the polygon causes me physical pain—the bullets fly through my body.

Eventually I look at myself—when the anger passes, which it does at some point—and see all the fears, pains and wounds in my reflection. What a good mirror you were! How scared I was of loneliness! So much so that I was willing to endure humiliation and shame, believing that I deserved it. To make it look like nothing happened the day after, make it non-existent, diminish problems to the size of insects. My first mirror was Mom, who with every cell in her body made me aware that I was a mistake, not fit for anything. I brought this twisted image of myself along with me to you, and you started to reflect it back to me. And I was so used to it, so convinced you were right. That I was right.

No one's right though, there is simply no such right. No one has the right to sow that kind of shame in anyone.

The drought's over. The storm's over. Droplets drip from the eaves, and the sun comes out and makes them shine. The water barrels are overflowing. The rain is soothing, especially when it starts letting up and the snails poke their heads out of their shells and delight in the moisture, and I put on my rubber boots and walk around in the garden to look at all this beauty. When it starts to rain again, I go back inside and cry a little more. It's just that kind of a rainy day.

Something about these insights is comforting. The fact that mornings are still beginnings, that the sun will still come out and that ultimately I only have to face my own fears. Sleep washed my anxiety away. I wake up in August, when everything is abundant. The plants are flourishing, the beet leaves are huge, the potato plants have grown to waist-height and are sagging everywhere, the lettuce has been blooming for a long time, and the sunflowers have grown taller than me. The tomatoes are about to collapse under their own weight. This lushness brings so much joy.

The letters I found in the closet were so full of longing, faith and desires, as well as things that would be difficult to say out loud. There's something hopeful in that. Maybe Elvi and I would have gotten along really well. I don't know why that thought makes me so happy. Maybe I want to identify with her, and feel like I'm following in someone's footsteps, treading a path. Tsõriksoo has made something sprout in me, that's for sure. Everything that broke inside me needed to be broken. The poison that was poured into me has come out painfully, with everything that I was made to believe about myself now bubbling to the surface and casting itself out. The belief that I can't take up space. Or be visible. Or need something. These knives don't scare me anymore. They're useless. They can just be twirled around and thrown, so that old men who want to decide over young women and their bodies lose their power of speech, and young men who expect women to be obedient and silent go blind. All your superiority deserves is contempt.

It rains stars at night. I sit on a garden chair wrapped in a thick quilt, in silence, staring at the sky. You can't always be sure if they're stars or satellites. I wonder why these old letters fascinate me and why I'm imagining someone else's past rather than my own future. What's to come is frightening, as frightening as the sudden painful explosions from the polygon. There's a hope that something might change, but I find it hard to believe in people, in benevolence. What can you trust? Whirlwinds come from the black sky, striking down trees and blowing away roofs. The constant rain rots the crops ripening in the fields. Yet I still trust the earth and the changeable weather and the crickets that won't stop singing any time soon. Yes, I find it hard to let people get close to me. But maybe that can be learned.

I write my sister an email. She's at her in-laws' cottage somewhere in Viljandi County and invites me to visit. I balk at the idea at first, but then I reconsider. I have to suppress the awkward feeling that I don't belong anywhere and that I'm not wanted. If she's inviting me, I have to believe it's genuine. Pille is younger than me but has two small children. A courageous person.

When I turn into their yard a couple of days later, I immediately start regretting it. The neatly trimmed lawn is intimidating. Respectable people live here. But I can't turn around anymore. I take the cake I bought from the store in Tsooru, and go inside.

After a tour of the house and garden, we sit on a spacious veranda overlooking the sauna and a small pond. Pille's wearing a colorful summer dress and runs around, makes coffee, offers pie. She looks good. Her husband's a salesman, a cheerful bald-headed guy. The older child is three, while the younger one will soon be a year old, already toddling around, but still smelling like milk. I'm embarrassed I didn't bring anything for the kids.

They don't need anything. They shouldn't start expecting every guest to bring gifts, my sister reassures me.

And then, with a certain bitterness, she says her husband's parents are already spoiling the children. And that our mother, who keeps talking about what a proud grandmother she is, hasn't visited this summer.

Our mom, who has been complaining to me for ages that I have no children.

I look at my sister and a memory stirs of helping her sharpen pencils almost every night. How she became more and more guarded with every new school year, just like me. How she slept in my bed when she'd had a bad dream. How I would sometimes hit her when she got too sad because I couldn't stand it. I cried rarely and only in secret.

I don't want to hear anything about that old stuff, Pille says when I ask her if she's tried to talk to Mom about when we were kids.

I'm interested in the here and now. It's no use raking up the past. We've battled our way out of it. It could have been worse. We had a roof over our heads and never went hungry.

I can hear my mom's words behind my sister's.

Pille changes the subject and asks how I can even put up with being at Tsõriksoo. Isn't the noise from the polygon getting on your nerves? She rolls her eyes. I couldn't be there with the kids. They'd be frightened and that one would wake up at every crunch, it's so hard to get her to sleep. Their neighbors are pretty far off, but if someone turns on a lawnmower somewhere, naptime is over. We need to tiptoe around here when she's sleeping.

It's not time for sleeping yet. Anna's in her mother's lap trying to grab things off the table, while three-year-old Robert is indoors with his grandmother.

We take a sauna. Little Anna is washed and handed over to her father. Robert with his blond curls stays with us and splashes water on our heads with a tablespoon. Pille and I take turns to go dipping in the pond.

Do you remember how we used to play on the hay bales until sunset?

In June.

The pond at Tsõriksoo is so overgrown now you can't swim in it. The ladder's been gone for a long time anyway.

The roof's still holding up?

Uh-huh.

You should come and see.

Come on a weekend, it'll be quieter. It'd be nice.

It would be.

Back at home. When I'm away from home, I call hotel rooms home too. But still: at home.

You could put up a greenhouse here. There's a big shed, full of junk. In fact, I could rent a trailer and get it all out from under the arch over the weekend. Clear away the dirt, cover it with plastic sheeting, and lay soil there in the spring. I could start growing tomato plants in the city, too. If the summers carry on being like this, the tomatoes in the garden will get water-logged and turn to mush; they'd be much better off in a greenhouse. I could test out different varieties. I could still call in an excavator to clear out the pond. I don't need a neat and tidy garden where there's not a single weed. That's exactly what I don't want. But it would be good for the frogs if they could swim in the pond. And I'd like to jump in sometimes.

I can even imagine myself as an amphibian. Spending some time in the city and some in the country. I'm a bit nervous about going back into town, but I wouldn't survive the winter here. Although maybe Pille's right, maybe I am too conciliatory and maybe I should find a more peaceful place, because here I can't shake off the feeling that I'm living in the middle of a war. Maybe I'm too willing to suffer and be content with just a little? But I don't have the money to buy a nice summer home. I can't afford to renovate an old house alone in a strange place. Having enough for a deposit on an apartment in town would already be pretty good. I could try and find some boring but more lucrative job, and sit out a couple of years in an office and save.

Or go somewhere different. Somewhere really different. I once had the idea of going abroad to university. I still could. Learn something new, something more than editing texts.

I look at the wind seeking its lost cradle inside the blades of grass. I'm moving through the summer like a lone traveler. The afternoon sun tires me out, and I nod off. When I wake up the sun's moved away and a cool tremor runs along my arms, gentler than a caress. The new moon's already in the sky and my mint tea has gone cold.

I get out of bed, slowly and reluctantly, like a plume of smoke unfurling. There's a crashing sound everywhere, but it's not thunderstorms making all this noise—it's bombs. The living room's already aflame, the acrid smoke scratches my throat. Now it's actually happening, a full strike on the house, I just about manage to think. Half the roof caves in before my eyes, and it's not just flames eating it, worms are twisting and devouring the roof and walls of the house with ever-larger fiery tongues. I need to get out, out, out. The fire blazes outside and the horizon is glowing. It's like a labyrinth, except I don't know if I'm at the entrance or the exit. Has the war started? Where to run, what to do? The only thing I've taken from the house is gardening gloves, I don't even know why, but now that I've got them, I just have to put them on.

I look around me. Everything's on fire.

I should run, but my legs won't move. They're rooted to the spot.

It's strange that although so much has changed in the last few months, I still have the feeling that I'm walking in place, that I'm frozen. Does this feeling come from inside me or outside? Is it even possible to lose the pressure to perform? The social media stories of my friends and acquaintances are full of new trips, experiences and companions. I have nothing to offer in return. I feel like a loser.

I put on my rubber boots and take my basket with me. I'm going for a wander in the forest to see if there are any mushrooms. Right behind the house, about five hundred meters away, is a chanterelle patch. A few weeks ago there was nothing there, but it's rained so much in the meantime. Even on the way there, I see several boletus, some of the bigger ones worm-eaten. A couple of spongy specimens end up in my basket. I don't know any mushrooms apart from chanterelles and boletus. Oh, and yellow russulas, we used to pick them when we were kids and they don't need parboiling. Our few hectares of forest are filled with fallen and decaying trees and the aspen leaves have formed a soft dark-brown carpet. The neighbor's forest is a little higher up and has lots of stumps; sometimes he cuts wood. You can tell straight away when you're over there, there's more light in his forest and the undergrowth is mossier. To be perfectly honest, the chanterelle patch is in the neighbor's forest. But that's always been the case. I don't know if anyone else has ever picked mushrooms here.

Anyway. There they are, the golden beauties. Between the yellow mushrooms are a couple of chewed fly agarics. The mushrooms are a little waterlogged, but that's okay. Before I put the chanterelles in the basket, I take a picture of them. The sunny forest is so beautiful. The smallest ones, I leave to grow. The basket's full anyway.

Back home, I create a post and wait. In the meantime, I start scrolling elsewhere, which is not such a bad idea, as it turns out, because I manage to score myself an apartment in town. It's only for four months, but that's enough. Someone I know is spending a semester abroad and renting out their apartment in the center, temporarily and pretty cheaply. I arrange to go and visit it in a few days.

The mushroom pictures get plenty of likes.

For a while, being in town unsettles me. I think I recognize him from behind. It takes a few seconds before I realize it's not actually Tarmo. Eugh. What am I actually afraid of? Not of him, really, but the power he had over me. Of how well he knew me and my weak points, and that he would force me back to a place I haven't wanted to be in a long time. Of not being able to stay calm. It's summer, so town is full of people buzzing in the pavement cafes, phones clicking and filming. The atmosphere is carefree, no one's in a hurry. I stand in a long queue for ice cream and watch two excited five- or six-year-old girls change their minds every two seconds about which ice cream to buy. Sooner or later, I'll bump into him, this town's too small to avoid it. If I want to live here, I have to be ready.

The apartment I'm moving into at the beginning of September is tasteful and spacious, with a view of the park. It has wooden floors, a large comfortable sofa, a fireplace and some paintings on the walls. It seems like a nice place and I'm as excited as the kids in the ice cream queue. Four months seems like a long time now, like a whole year. When the new year arrives, we'll see what happens, and how. But I don't need to patch up my life with duct tape anymore. My legs are strong from the groundwork, and I'm not as easily bowed.

At least that's what I'd like to think. And why shouldn't it be true?

In the evening, Silja was on Messenger, still exhilarated by the festivals she'd been to.

yes so it's a waste of money. but what else is there to do in the summer?

stay quietly in one place instead of moving around the whole time?

sure but it gets weird in town. and I know I'll always want to go someplace anyway

mmh well I didn't really go anywhere

didn't get bored?

I did a little bit and then it passed. I wasn't about to drive around for ages and live it up in tents. too old for that now

I know. some of the live shows were pretty cool though and the parties were crazy. I don't regret it. it's fun with your own gang

sure. maybe next summer I'll go to a few

ok and I'll come visit you in the country if you're there. sorry I didn't make it this time

no worries

I don't know how I get caught in the same trap every year. always having to go from one event to another or sleep something off. well I actually KNOW what happens. in the middle of winter depression, I convince myself that these tickets have to be bought because in summer it's so nice to chill with friends at a festival in the back of beyond where the burgers cost at least ten euros

well I'm thinking again why are we led to believe that we have to have some kind of companion? that if you're alone then it's only because you can't find anyone. oh poor me, I'm alone, but I'm also totally whole... I don't have to hang out with some guy just because otherwise I'd be alone come on look at me, delighted to be single for two years. there have been a few encounters in the meantime, but I wouldn't want to live with them. mom just asked me if I'm a lesbian. she says I can tell her, she's open to it. god

really? that's cringe

I know! I was like mom, dear, I'm single on purpose don't worry about me everything's fine

The afternoon is dead time. Drowsy and blunt. Thoughts get stuck and I have no desire to do anything, it all seems too difficult. Tired, but don't want to sleep. Bored, but can't manage to do anything. Usually it helps to do a bit of weeding in the garden, but the weather is bleak and windy. I look for music that softens things, a nice vibe that can lift me out of this indifference. I put on some percussive music. Suddenly I start dancing, just like that. The rhythms are fast and dark and the movement comes by itself, as if something had been waiting for a way out at just this time, this too-calm moment before the arrival of the evening when the clocks threaten to stop. But this rhythm is impossible to resist: my knees bend, my back straightens, my shoulders begin to move and set my body going, the same body that remembers something from a summer and fall a few years back when I went to dance classes. My legs sweep up specks of dust, warm dust from a distant desert, and my hands cut corn with machetes: they cut off ripe yellow heads, cut off all obstacles, all chains, anything that binds me to the old. It's the dance of the goddess of thunder and storms, who can destroy and create, who makes it rain and who leads the souls of the dead to the other side; the dance of the invincible war queen, sweet and sour, triumphant, soft but determined. Legs, shoulders, back and belly button, hips, neck and skin. And I dance like the wind that breathes out words that were never permitted to be spoken before. And I dance like a storm that pushes away everything that's no longer needed, a storm that bends trees to the ground, one that destroys. And I dance like water flowing softly and carving new paths and frontiers, into stone if necessary. And I breathe and I sweat and I'm glad I have a body that moves, jumps, stretches, reaches up high, and keeps me on the ground and rooted.

When Mom calls, I'm working. I'm editing a book where the terms are utterly mixed up.

Hello? Hi. Now it's started.

What has?

What we've all been waiting for. And how things will be divided …

What? What's happening? Please tell me.

My mother gives a loud sigh. I got a letter yesterday, and so did Tiina. From the Center for Defense Investments. You see?

What do they want? What am I supposed to see here?

It's being expropriated.

No … You can't be serious. We can't give up Tsõriksoo. It can't be possible. Why now?

I don't know why now. But it's happening. And we also have to get a lawyer, because the amount they've put here is ridiculously small.

How much is it?

Sixty thousand. I mean, come on. They want to pay sixty thousand for the memories of several generations. As compensation! We need to discuss it. It's pocket money for them.

Is there a way of not selling? Maybe we should fight for our house, instead of just giving up.

And then let it be expropriated without compensation? Well, that's a clever idea. Besides, you're going back to town anyway. You're there one summer, and you think you're a farmer? The house is falling apart, that's a fact. Are you going to build there? I don't think so, do you? There's no one with the energy to fix it up.

I thought I could do something here …

The turkey thought, too. Live next to the polygon? Who was it complaining about having to spend days indoors instead of outdoors because there was so much shooting going on? It hasn't been a quiet place in a long time. There's a war going on!

What about the forest? Will it get chopped down?

How would I know. If they have to. It's none of our business anymore. I'm not going to touch the forest. But I want a hundred grand for that house, nothing less. Either way, we'll have to split it with Tiina. Ha! Sixty thousand, what do they take me for?

When will the sale take place?

I don't know. First I'll get a lawyer. But you're going back to town soon anyway. Tiina and I will sort these things out. We can sell off what's in the house first. Is there anything you need, furniture or dishes or something? For the new place.

I don't think I do to start with. I'll be renting and it has everything.

You can still take the knives and forks. And the dishes, let's see. Anyway, I hope we'll be done by the new year. We'll ask for at least a few months to move out. The house and shed are full of stuff. But it depends on the military, of course.

Aren't you upset?

Me? No. Honestly, it's good to be rid of it. We can celebrate Midsummer in town with a bonfire. Or let's go to Pille's or something. We'll see. No one has the time or energy to keep that old decaying house in order.

It's like I'm working in a fog. I reread the sentences several times because my thoughts keep wandering. I'm trying to keep tuned in to the here and now. But somewhere below the surface, the knowledge pulsates away. There won't be another summer here.

So many questions. Where are they going to extend the polygon now? Will the whole village vanish in a new extension? Are the neighbors selling up?

I go visit my neighbor to find out what he knows. I discover I don't have anything to bring except a spare packet of cookies in the closet.

Jaanus is mowing the lawn just the other side of the sauna. When he notices me, he switches it off, apologizes for being so sweaty and leaves me outside while he goes indoors to put on a dry shirt.

I sit on a garden chair and look around. I notice a small chicken yard next to the shed where the birds are scratching around. The storm has caused more damage here than at our place. Jaanus tries to offer me coffee or another drink, but I insist on a glass of water.

He brings two glasses of water and opens the cookies.

So I was just wondering if you'd been told about the expropriation?

A serious expression appears on his face and he sits down.

Yeah, I was. And so were you, then. That's it for us.

So what will you do? Do you have somewhere to move to?

I don't know yet. Jesus, it's like deportation, driving us out of our homes. I'm not going anywhere for now.

I'll get the deadline extended if I can. If I have to, I'll sue.

But then if you end up getting expropriated, you'll still lose the house and get less money.

Ah, says Jaanus, waving a hand and looking away. It's all the same to me. Maybe I'll think about it over the winter. There's too much else to do right now.

What about your chickens?

Whatever happens, they all end up in soup sooner or later.

Who else has had a letter? The whole village?

As far as I've heard, it's all the way to Savilõõvi. But I don't know if this will become the danger zone or if the bastards will be bombing the garden here later.

I don't know either. This time it hasn't even been on the news.

Some reporters were there with a camera. It'll be on the news. But what good is it?

None, I guess. But it would be strange if there was no reaction.

That's all Jaanus has to say about it. Instead he shows me where the storm pulled a bush out by the roots, leaving a hole behind.

When I leave, he gives me a box of eggs and a bag of cucumbers.

Pickle them or eat them fresh. Life will carry on somehow.

The color of the marigolds is absolutely crazy, my eyes are brimming with orange and yellow. The wasps that appeared out of nowhere are yellow too: hungry, vicious creatures rushing at the plate when I eat outside. But the mosquitoes are gone.

My instinct is to fight, but whom? My mom? The government? The military? It wouldn't do any good.

The end of summer is on the horizon. August is full-bodied, overgrown and warm. The evenings getting cool, the dew collecting on the ground early. Fall is drawing in everywhere. So early! Even the light is different: softer, more conciliatory.

Am I different, am I more my own?

I've set new boundaries, but can I protect them?

The reflection of the first knife I dreamed of is in my hand again. It's a small, articulated knife. The blade's sharp, ready to protect me if necessary.

I've always tried to forgive myself for things I didn't do. For the fog that descends in the morning, for the shadows that first grow, then shrink. This cold ghostly guilt has followed me all my life: the guilt of being myself. The pale beauty of my harsh childhood. The rigid plastic taste of stencils.

I know that there's no way out of the pain, that the fear will remain and squeeze me in its icy arms, but now I'm ready to look you straight in the eye and tell you: You no longer have any power. You're in the past.

All this cow parsley will keep swaying here and soon enough—not this fall and perhaps not the next, but still, fairly soon—it will merge with the landscape of the green-roofed house. Nature will take over and erase human traces. Not everything I've started to appreciate will be lost, of course. The oak tree will remain, the young birches will grow large, the aspens will keep on flickering and the apple trees will run wild, but possibly still bear fruit. The house will still be here, at least to start with. As long as the roof holds. When it no longer does, rain and snow will do their work and enter the rooms, infiltrate the hundred-year-old logs. Gradually the walls will collapse and the rooms will fill with greenery. It could actually be a pretty sight: instead of my bed, a room full of nettles.

There are some old farmsteads in this village, and some that only exist in name and at most some memories and stories—and, of course, veteran trees. The cottages collapse but the trees remain. And that's the way it should be. But up until now there were also houses where people lived alongside these dilapidated farmhouses. Now the whole village seems to be disappearing. This area is going to be lifeless. Sometimes a fox runs through the yard, but there are fewer and fewer animals around here. And the birds can hardly enjoy the noise of war.

The insects, though, they'll stay. Perhaps Tsõriksoo will eventually become an ant kingdom for real.

The cranes on the far side of the field are already calling a metallic-sounding farewell, the sound of them preparing to fly away.

On the last night I slowly pack my things. There isn't much. For a moment I consider whether or not to take Elvi's letters, but then I decide that they belong to the house, and I return them to the back of the closet.

The creaks of the old house are like silent prayers.

I'd planned to go back to town anyway, but I didn't expect it to be so final. Now every moment is the last, and I desperately want to record everything. I take pictures, and when it seems like there's no point in taking any more, I sit and try to remember what's not in the pictures. The brightness of the birches, the sun setting behind the trees, the dancing of small insects in the yellow light, the sky and clouds that glisten unlike in any other place. I sit in the garden chair until it gets dark.

I haven't got the heart to move, I don't want to move.

The sheet metal that covers the woodpile is rattling in the wind. The hooded crow sways on the oak tree and caws. The quiet murmur of the clover and the golden silence of the mayweed. They sing inside me as if my innermost being is the center of everything, both living and dead.

I'm between two worlds and don't belong to one or the other just yet: neither night nor day, dream nor reality, country nor city, ground nor sky.

But here I am in spite of all that.

I'm swaying on the cut line that separates my previous life from what's to come. I might lean a little in one direction and then the other, but the cut line will allow me a little space. A few days, a week or a month to get myself together. And then with a quick strong tug—rip!

I can try to convince myself I'll be back here again. But who am I trying to kid? I'm not going to start carrying things away from here, that's someone else's job. In my memories, this place will remain just the way it was this morning—perfect and calm, undisturbed at the age of a hundred.

Tsõriksoo will stand proudly for as long as it is allowed to.

I lock the door and heave the last things into the car. The few words I have left are hovering in the air. The wind is warm and caresses my shoulders like a distant friend. Going away always stings, because the road can take you anywhere. The clouds cast soft shadows over the landscape. And then there's the sound of a gunshot, and I lift my eyes like a startled bird.

DARCY HURFORD translates from Swedish, Finnish, and Estonian into English. Originally from England, she is now based in Belgium, where she has been working for around twelve years. She studied modern languages at the University of East Anglia and comparative literature at Åbo Akademi University in Finland. Her translations have appeared in *Asymptote* and *Ellipse Magazine*.

Book Club Discussion Guides on our website.

World Editions promotes voices from around the globe by publishing books from many different countries and languages in English translation. Through our work, we aim to enhance dialogue between cultures, foster new connections, and open doors which may otherwise have remained closed.

Also available from World Editions:

Breakwater
Marijke Schermer
Translated by Liz Waters
A novel about a marriage torn apart by a violent secret
for fans of Lauren Groff's *Fates and Furies*
"Excellent novel. Packed with emotional truth and
elegantly turned narrative." —Ian McEwan, author
of international bestseller *Atonement*

My Mother Says
Stine Pilgaard
Translated by Hunter Simpson
"Reeling from a breakup, a young Danish woman
recovers her sense of self through conversations with
parents, friends, and strangers. A sweet and quirky
debut about heartbreak, memory, and the endless
potential of language." —*Kirkus Reviews*

Where the Wind Calls Home
Samar Yazbek
Translated by Leri Price
2024 NATIONAL BOOK AWARD FINALIST
"Samar Yazbek's spellbinding novel tells the story of
Ali—a wounded soldier holding on to life during the
Syrian civil war." —National Book Award Jury

Abyss
Pilar Quintana
Translated by Lisa Dillman
2023 NATIONAL BOOK AWARD FINALIST
"A triumph of perception and representation."
—National Book Award Jury

On the Design

As book design is an integral part of the reading experience, we would like to acknowledge the work of those who shaped the form in which the story is housed.

Tessa van der Waals (Netherlands) is responsible for the cover design, cover typography, and art direction of all World Editions books. She works in the internationally renowned tradition of Dutch Design. Her bright and powerful visual aesthetic maintains a harmony between image and typography, and captures the unique atmosphere of each book. She works closely with internationally celebrated photographers, artists, and letter designers. Her work has frequently been awarded prizes for Best Dutch Book Design.

When designing a typographical cover, the biggest pitfall for a designer is to visualize the literal meaning of a book. For the title, Tessa van der Waals chose fonts from Broker, an angular display type family designed to make a statement. She captured the feel of *The Cut Line* by stacking two different styles (Sans and Stressed) horizontally and vertically. Broker is designed by In-House International, a boundary-pushing creative studio and type foundry based in Austin, Texas. The author's name is set in the typeface Eagle, designed by David Berlow (Fontbureau) and selected for its unique kind of boldness. The emerald green was a very deliberate choice, too. It's a type of green not found in nature, though nature plays a key role in the book.

Euan Monaghan (United Kingdom) is responsible for the typography and careful interior book design.

The text on the inside covers and the press quotes are set in Circular, designed by Laurenz Brunner (Switzerland) and published by Swiss type foundry Lineto.

All World Editions books are set in the typeface Dolly, specifically designed for book typography. Dolly creates a warm page image perfect for an enjoyable reading experience. This typeface is designed by Underware, a European collective formed by Bas Jacobs (Netherlands), Akiem Helmling (Germany), and Sami Kortemäki (Finland). Underware are also the creators of the World Editions logo, which meets the design requirement that "a strong shape can always be drawn with a toe in the sand."